Holly looked at his grimly set mouth and the dark shadow of sexy stubble that surrounded it. The clench of his jaw suggested he was only just holding on to his temper.

Her heart began to thump—but not out of fear. It wasn't Julius she was afraid of but her reaction to him. She had never felt her body react in this way. His touch triggered something raw and primal in her. She had never felt her body *ache*. Pulse and contract with a longing she couldn't describe because she had never felt it quite like this before. She wasn't a virgin, but none of her few sexual encounters had made her flesh sing like this. He hadn't even kissed her and yet she felt as if she was on a knife-edge. Every nerve in her body was standing up and waiting. Anticipating. Wanting. *Hungering.*

And then he suddenly dropped his hands from her arms. The movement was so unexpected she nearly toppled backwards into the pool, but somehow managed to regain her balance. She maintained her composure—*just*—with a cool look cast his way.

'One thing you should note,' she said. 'I *don't* take orders. Not from you or from anyone.'

The Ravensdale Scandals

Scandal is this family's middle name!

With notoriously famous parents, the Ravensdale
children grew up in the limelight. But *nothing* could
have prepared them for this latest scandal…
the revelation of a Ravensdale love-child!

London's most eligible siblings find themselves
in the eye of their own paparazzi storm.
They're determined to fight back—
they just never factored in falling in love too…!

Find out what happens in
Julius Ravensdale's story
Ravensdale's Defiant Captive
December 2015

Miranda Ravensdale's story
Awakening the Ravensdale Heiress
January 2016

And watch for Jake and Katherine's
Ravensdale Scandals…coming soon!

RAVENSDALE'S DEFIANT CAPTIVE

BY
MELANIE MILBURNE

First published in Great Britain 2015
by Mills & Boon, an imprint of Harlequin (UK) Limited,
Eton House, 18-24 Paradise Road, Richmond, Surrey, TW9 1SR

© 2015 Melanie Milburne

ISBN: 978-0-263-26054-0

An avid romance reader, **Melanie Milburne** loves writing the kind of books that gave her so much joy as she was busy getting married to her own hero and raising a family. Now a *USA TODAY* bestselling author, she has won several awards—including The Australian Readers' Association most popular category/series romance in 2008 and the prestigious Romance Writers of Australia R*BY award in 2011.

She loves to hear from readers!

MelanieMilburne.com.au
Facebook.com/Melanie.Milburne
Twitter @MelanieMilburn1

Books by Melanie Milburne

Mills & Boon Modern Romance

At No Man's Command
His Final Bargain
Uncovering the Silveri Secret
Surrendering All But Her Heart
His Poor Little Rich Girl

The Chatsfield

Chatsfield's Ultimate Acquisition

The Playboys of Argentina

The Valquez Bride
The Valquez Seduction

Those Scandalous Caffarellis

Never Say No to a Caffarelli
Never Underestimate a Caffarelli
Never Gamble with a Caffarelli

The Outrageous Sisters

Deserving of His Diamonds?
Enemies at the Altar

Visit the Author Profile page at
millsandboon.co.uk for more titles.

To Ella Carey,
a talented writer, a dear friend and a wonderful person.
I love our writing chats! xxx

CHAPTER ONE

JULIUS RAVENSDALE KNEW his housekeeper was up to something as soon as she brought in his favourite dessert. 'Queen's pudding?' He raised one of his brows. 'I never have dessert at lunch unless it's a special occasion.'

'It *is* a special occasion,' Sophia said as she put the meringue-topped dessert in front of him.

He narrowed his gaze. 'Okay, tell me. What's going on?'

Sophia's expression was sheepish. 'I'm bringing in a girl to help me run the house. It's only for a month until this wretched tendonitis settles. The extra pair of hands will be so helpful and I'll be doing my bit for society. It's a win-win.'

Julius glanced at the wrist brace Sophia had been wearing for the past couple of weeks. He knew she worked far too hard and could do with the extra help but he liked to keep the staff numbers down in the villa. Not because he was mean about paying them. He would pay them triple to stay away and let him get on with his work. 'Who is it?'

'Just a girl who's in need of a bit of direction.'

Julius mentally rolled his eyes. Of all the housekeepers he could have chosen, he had employed the Argentinian reincarnation of Mother Teresa. 'I thought we agreed your lame ducks were restricted to the stables or the gardens?'

'I know, but this girl will go to prison if—'

'Prison?' he said. 'You're bringing a convicted criminal here?'

'She's only been in trouble a couple of times,' Sophia said. 'Anyway, maybe the guy deserved it.'

'What did she do to him?'

'She keyed his brand-new sports car.'

Julius's gut clenched at the thought of his showroom-perfect Aston Martin housed in the garage. 'I suppose she said it was an accident?'

'No, she admitted to it,' Sophia said. 'She was proud of it. That and the message she sprayed on his lawn with weed killer.'

'She sounds delightful.'

'So you'll agree to have her?'

Julius took in his housekeeper's hopeful expression. His sarcasm was lost on her. Sophia was the most charitable person he knew. Always doing things for others. Always looking for a way to make a difference in someone's life. He knew she was lonely since both her adult children had moved abroad for work. What would it hurt to indulge her just this once? He would be busy with fine-tuning his space software. He had less than a month to iron out the kinks in the programming before he presented it to the research team for funding approval.

He let out a long breath. 'I don't suppose you've ever thought of taking up knitting or cross-stitch instead?'

Sophia beamed at him. 'Just wait until you meet her. You're going to love her.'

* * *

Holly considered making a run for it when the van stopped but the size of the villa and its surrounds made her pause. It was big. Way big. Massive. It probably had its own area code. Maybe its own political party. It was four storeys high, built in a neo-classical style with spectacular gardens and lush, rolling fields fringed by thick forest. It didn't look anything like the detention centre she'd envisaged. There was no twelve-foot-high fence with electrified barbed wire at the top. There was no surveillance tower and no uniformed, rifle-toting guards—or, at least, none she could see—casing the joint. It looked like a top-end hotel—a luxurious and very private resort for the rich and famous. Which kind of made her wonder why she'd been sent here. Not that she'd been expecting chains and bread and water or anything, but still. This was seriously over the top.

'It's only for a month,' Natalia Varela, her case-worker, said as the decorative wrought-iron gates opened electronically, allowing them access to the long, sweeping limestone driveway leading to the immaculately maintained villa. 'You got off lightly considering your rap sheet. I know a few people who'd happily swap places with you.'

Holly grunted. Folded her arms across her breasts. Crossed her right leg over her left. Jerked her ankle up and down. Pouted. Why should she look happy? Why should she act *grateful* that she was being sent to live with some man she'd never heard of in his big, old fancy villa?

A month.

Thirty-one days of living with some stranger who

had magnanimously volunteered to 'reform' her. Ha-
ha. Like that was going to work. Who was this guy
anyway? All she'd been told was he was some hotshot
techie nerd from England who had made the big time in
Argentina designing software for space telescopes used
in the Atacama Desert in neighbouring Chile. Oh, and
he was apparently single. Holly rolled her eyes. He'd
agreed to take on a troubled young woman for altruistic reasons? And the correctional authorities had actually *fallen* for that?

Yeah, right. She knew all about men and their dodgy
motivations.

After being given the all clear from the security in-
tercom device, Natalia drove through the gates before
they whispered shut behind the car. 'Julius Ravensdale
is doing you a big favour,' she said. 'He's only agreed to
this—and very reluctantly at that—because his housekeeper has tendonitis in her wrist. You'll be her right-
hand helper. It's an amazing opportunity. This place is
like a five-star resort. It'll be great vocational training
for you. I hope you'll make the most of it.'

Vocational training for what? Holly thought with
a cynical curl of her lip. No one was going to make a
housekeeper out of her just because she'd made a few
mistakes, which weren't even really mistakes, because
her pond-scum stepfather had seriously had it coming
to him. It was just a dumb old sports car, for pity's sake.
So what if he had to have it re-sprayed and his precious
lawn re-sown after the weedkiller incident?

Holly was not going to be some rich man's lowly
slave scrubbing floors until her knees grew callouses
as big as cabbages. Her days of being pushed around
were long over. Julius Ravens-whatever-his-name-was

would be in for a big shock if he thought he could exploit her to suit his nefarious needs.

What if it wasn't the kitchen he planned to have her slaving in? What if he had more salacious plans? In her experience, men with money thought they could have anything and anyone they wanted. All that nonsense about him 'reluctantly' agreeing to take her on was just a ruse. Of course he would say that. He wouldn't want to look *too* eager to take in a prison statistic waiting to happen. He would be 'doing his bit for society' by trying to *do her*.

Bring it on, she thought. *Let's see how far you get.*

'Oh, I'll make the most of it, all right,' Holly said as she sent the caseworker a guileless smile. 'You can be sure of that.'

Natalia let out a world-weary sigh as she put her foot back on the accelerator. 'Yeah, that's what I'm afraid of.'

The housekeeper whom she had met a few days before greeted Holly at the door of the villa while Natalia took an urgent call from one of her other charges.

'It's lovely to have you here, Holly,' Sophia said. 'Come in. Señor Ravensdale is busy just now so I'll show you to your suite so you can settle in.'

Holly wasn't expecting a welcoming committee with banners and balloons and a brass band or anything but surely the very least her host could do was make an appearance? If he'd agreed to have her here then he could at least do the polite thing and greet her face to face. 'Where is he?' she asked.

'He's not to be disturbed,' Sofia said. 'I'll show you to the suite I've pre—'

'Disturb him, please,' Holly said. *'Now.'*

Sophia looked a little taken aback. 'He doesn't like to be interrupted while he's working. He doesn't allow anyone into his office unless it's an emergency.'

Holly gently elbowed her way past to the door she took to be the study. It was the only door that was closed along the long, wide corridor. She didn't knock. She turned the handle and barged in.

A man looked up from behind a desk where he was tapping at a computer keyboard. His fingers stalled as she came in, the last click echoing in the silence as his gaze met with hers.

Holly drew in a breath to speak but for some reason her voice wasn't on active duty. It had locked behind her shock at how different he was from her expectations. He was nothing like she had envisaged. He wasn't old or even middle-aged. He was in his early thirties and movie-star handsome, athletically lean and tanned. His hair was a rich dark brown with light waves running through it. It looked as if it had been recently styled with his fingers, for she could see the roughly spaced plough marks that gave him a sexily tousled look, as if he'd just tumbled out of bed after vigorous sex. He had a deter-mined looking jaw, a straight nose and a firm but sen-sually sculptured mouth that for some reason made the ligaments at the backs of her knees weaken alarmingly.

He pushed back his chair, and the room instantly shrank as he stood. 'Can I help you?' he said with the sort of tone that suggested he was not in the least mo-tivated to do so.

Holly had never been one to beat about the bush. Her tactic was to get in there with a verbal weed-whacker. 'Don't you know it's impolite to ignore your guests when they arrive?'

His eyes held hers with steely focus. 'Strictly speaking, you're not my guest. You're Sophia's.'

Holly hitched up her chin, flashing him an I-know-what-you're-up-to glare. 'I want to let you know straight from the outset I'm not here to be your sex toy.'

His dark brows rose in twin arcs over his impossibly dark blue eyes. With his black hair and olive-skinned complexion, she had been expecting them to be brown. But they were an astonishing sapphire-blue fringed with thick black lashes. He seemed to measure her for a moment; his gaze taking in the tiny diamond nose piercing and the pink streaks in her hair with a tilt of his mouth that was unmistakably mocking.

A knot of bitterness inside Holly tightened. If there was one thing she loathed, it was being made fun of. Belittled. Mocked.

'How do you do, Miss, er...?' He glanced at his housekeeper, who had come in behind Holly, for a prompt.

'Miss Perez,' Sophia said. 'Hollyanne.'

'Holly,' Holly said with a black look.

Julius offered his hand. 'How do you do, Holly?'

She glared at his hand as if he'd just offered her a viper. 'Keep your hands to yourself.'

Natalia entered his office sounding a little flustered. 'I'm terribly sorry, Dr Ravensdale, but I had to take an urgent call about another client—'

Holly swung around and frowned at Natalia. '*Doctor*? You didn't tell me he was a doctor. You said he was a computer geek.'

The caseworker gave Julius a pained smile before addressing Holly. 'Dr Ravensdale has a PhD in astrophysics. It's polite to call him by his correct title, if that's what he prefers.'

Holly swung back to look at Julius. 'What do you want me to call you? Sir? Master? Oh Mighty Learned One? Your Royal Tightness?'

His lips twitched as if he was fighting back a reluctant smile. 'Julius will be fine.'

'As in Caesar?'

'As it turns out, yes.'

'You're into Shakespeare?' Holly said it as if it was a noxious disease from which she had so far managed to escape contamination. No point letting him think she was anything but what he had already judged her as: uneducated and unsophisticated. Trailer trash.

'No, but my parents are.'

'Why'd you agree to have me here?' she said, eye-balling him.

'I didn't want you here,' he said. 'But my current domestic circumstances made it impossible for me to refuse.'

Holly folded her arms across her chest. 'I can't cook,' she said with an obdurate 'so what are you going to do about *that*?' look.

'I'm sure you can learn.'

'And I hate housework,' she said. 'It's sexist expecting women to clean up after you. Just because I've got boobs and ovaries doesn't mean I—'

'Point taken,' he said quickly. So quickly Holly wondered if he was worried she was going to list all of her feminine assets. 'However, you need to do your stint of community service,' he continued. 'I need some help around the house until Sophia gets better. It's win-win.'

Holly made a harrumphing noise and unwound her locked arms, turning her gaze to the caseworker. 'Have you done a police check on him to make sure he's the real deal?'

'I can assure you, Holly, Dr Ravensdale is a totally trustworthy guardian,' the caseworker said.

Holly pushed her bottom lip out like a drawer as she swung back to size Julius up. 'Do you drink?'

'Socially.'

'Smoke?'

'No.'

'Drugs?'

'No.'

Holly upped her brazenness another notch. 'Sex?'

'Holly…' the caseworker began.

'What?' Holly asked with a petulant scowl.

'You're embarrassing Dr Ravensdale.'

'I'm not embarrassed,' Julius said. 'But I'm also not going to answer such an impertinent question.'

Holly coughed out a laugh. 'Which means you're not getting any, right?'

He stared her down with a look that made her insides feel wobbly. He didn't look the type of man to go too long between drinks. He looked the type of man who could take his pick of women. She could feel his sensual allure like a force field. Her mind ran wild with images of him getting down to business. He wouldn't be one for a quick, sleazy grope. He would take his time. He would know his way around a woman's body. He would know how to send female senses spinning into the stratosphere. She could see it in the darkly confident glint of his gaze. 'While we're on the topic,' he said, 'I would appreciate it if you would abstain from bringing men here for the purpose of having intimate relations with them.'

'So…you get to have sex but I don't? That is…' Holly dropped her voice to a deliberately husky purr '…unless we have it with each other?'

'I have to get going,' the caseworker said as her phone buzzed with an incoming message. 'Holly, I hope you'll behave yourself while you're here. This is your last chance, don't forget. If this fails you know where you'll be going.'

'Yeah, yeah, yeah,' Holly said with a bored flicker of her eyelids as she turned to look at the view from one of the windows next to a wall of bookshelves. She didn't want to go to prison but neither did she want to be exploited by yet another man who assumed he had some sort of power over her. If Julius Ravensdale wanted a plaything, why hadn't he cut one from the herd? The herd he belonged to—the 'beautiful people' herd. She wasn't even his type. How could she be, with her cheap chain-store clothes? Not to mention her background. The background she was still trying to escape. It clung to her like thick axle grease. No amount of washing and cleansing and sanitising would remove it.

Julius Ravensdale came from money. She could see it in the way he dressed, in the way he held himself with supreme confidence, with cool and collected authority. She could see it in the furnishings he surrounded himself with: the priceless paintings, the books and the hand-woven floor coverings. He hadn't lived his childhood in sweat-soaked fear. He hadn't had to fight for survival. He'd had everything handed to him on a gilt-edged platter. Why was he agreeing to have her here if not to make use of her? She clenched her back teeth in determination. He would *not* use her.

She would use *him* first.

* * *

'I'll call each day to see how she's getting on,' the case-worker said to Julius as she shook his hand. 'It's very good of you to commit to this programme. It's helped many people turn their lives around.'

'I'm sure everything will be fine,' Julius assured her. 'Sophia will do most of the mentoring.'

'All the same, it's very kind of you to open your home like this.'

'It's a big house,' he said. *Maybe not big enough.*

Julius turned once Sophia had escorted the case-worker out of his office to find Holly looking at him with a flinty gaze. 'How much are they paying you to have me?' she said.

'I've told them to donate the fee to charity.'

'Big of you.'

He leaned against the windowsill behind his desk with his hands balanced either side of his hips to study her. It was a casual pose that belied the havoc her presence caused to his senses. He could feel the blood humming through his veins in a way it hadn't since he'd been a teenager. He looked down at her upturned, defiant face with its flashing caramel-brown gaze and sulky cherry-red mouth. A tiny diamond winked from the side of her right nostril. The bridge of her retroussé nose was dusted with freckles that reminded him of nutmeg sprinkled on top of a dessert. But that was about as far as he could go with the sweetness description. She looked sour and bitter and ready for a fight.

Something about her blatant rudeness made everything that was cultured in Julius stiffen. *Not, perhaps, the best choice of word*, he thought wryly as he scanned her impudent features. But her rudeness wasn't the only thing that was blatant about her. She had an earthy, raw sensuality about her. The way she moved her body. The way she inhabited her body. *His* body recognised it like a stallion scenting a potential mate.

He forced his mind out of the gutter. Clearly he needed to get some work-life balance if this little upstart was attracting his attention.

Her face was not what one would call classically beautiful but there was an arresting quality to it that made him want to study her for longer than was socially polite. He noted the high and haughty cheekbones you could slice a Christmas ham on. Eyelashes that were thick and long without the boost of mascara. Her skin—apart from the freckles and the diamond piercing—was creamy and make-up-free. Her hair was a mass of springy shoulder-length curls and was a mid shade of brown, apart from some rather vivid streaks of pink.

Julius was still waiting for her to make the connection between him and his parents. It didn't usually take this long. He had got used to it over the years. Well, almost: the wide-eyed wonder. The delighted shock that produced a sickening number of gushing comments: *Oh, you're the son of the famous London West End actors Richard Ravensdale and Elisabetta Albertini! Can you get me their autographs? An invitation to opening night? Front-row seats? A back-stage pass? An audition?*

But Miss Holly Perez had either never heard of his parents or was not impressed by his lineage.

Julius had to admit he found her forthrightness strangely appealing. It was such a refreshing change. He'd had his share of sycophants. People who only wanted to be associated with him because of his connection with London theatre royalty. Women who wanted to be squired by him on the red carpet in the hope of catching the eye of a casting agent. It was refreshing to be in the presence of someone who didn't give a toss for the shallowness of his parents' celebrity.

Julius didn't care too much for the word 'guardian' the caseworker had used in reference to him. It made him sound decades older than his thirty-three years. Holly was younger than him certainly but only by about seven or eight years at the most. Twenty-five, but hardened by her experiences. He could see it in her eyes. There was no sheen of innocence in that thickly fringed brown gaze. It was full of cold, hard cynicism. A mess-with-me-at-your-peril gleam. What had led her to a life of petty crime? He'd seen the list of her offences: theft; wilful damage to property; graffiti; vandalism.

Sophia's rescue mission was perhaps going to be a little more challenging than he'd bargained for. He'd agreed to it because he trusted his housekeeper's judgement. But Sophia's judgement was clearly not what it used to be. Holly had come striding in like a denim-and-cheap-cotton-clad whirlwind—asking him about his sex life, for God's sake.

He knew he was acting and sounding like a stern schoolmaster. But he figured it was best to get the ground rules in early. He wasn't going to stand by while Holly conducted drunken parties or all-night orgies under his roof.

Julius didn't care how many impertinent questions she asked, he wasn't going to admit to his current sex drought. He'd been busy. He was working on some new top-secret software. He wasn't like his twin brother, Jake, who had sex as if he were training for the Olympics. Nor was he like his father, who had a reputation as a womaniser that was regrettably well deserved.

Julius enjoyed the company of women. He dated from time to time. He enjoyed the physicality of sex but he didn't care for the politics of it. The agenda women brought to the bedroom irked him. If he wanted to marry and settle down, then he would make the decision when he was good and ready. Although he seriously wondered if he would ever be ready. Having witnessed his parents' turbulent marriage, acrimonious divorce, remarriage and ongoing drama-filled relationship, he wasn't sure he wanted to sign up for the potential for so much disruption and chaos.

'I know why you've agreed to have me here, so don't bother pretending otherwise.' Holly's look had a bad-girl gleam to it that messed with his hormones. He felt a stirring in his groin. A lightning flash of unbidden lust that made his blood throb and pound in his veins. He was surprised—and deeply annoyed—by his reaction to her. She was obviously well aware of her effect on the male gaze, exploiting it for all it was worth. Her unusual beauty, even though it was currently downplayed, was the sort that could stop a bullet train in its tracks. She had a sensual air about her. A way of moving her body that made him ache to see what she looked like naked. He kept his expression masked but he wondered if she sensed the impact she had on him.

How had he got himself into this? Julius thought. He should have called an agency. Employed someone who had credentials. Someone who had training. Manners. Decorum. Why had he allowed Sophia to talk him into taking on someone as cheeky and wilful as Holly Perez? She was going to be living under his roof. For a month!

'You are mistaken, Miss Perez,' he said coolly. 'My taste in women is far more sophisticated.'

She adopted a femme fatale pose, all slinky hips and shoulders, her mouth in a come-and-get-me moue. 'Of course it is,' she said with a devilish little twinkle that matched the diamond in her nose.

Julius felt the swell of his flesh at her brazen sexuality. The pounding and purring of his blood drove every rational thought out of his brain. Sex was suddenly all he could think about. Hot, sweaty, bed-wrecking sex. Mind-blowing caveman sex. Driving himself into her tight, wet warmth and exploding like a bomb. How long had it been? Clearly too long if he was getting jumpy at this outrageous little flirt. Holly Perez was a trouble-maker. It might as well be branded across her forehead. He wasn't going to fall for it. He was not at the mercy of his hormones...or at least he hadn't been before now.

Holly moved around his office with cat-like grace. Slinky, silent, sensuous. Dangerous, if stroked the wrong way. Although when he checked he noticed she didn't have claws. Her fingernails were bitten down to the quick. When she lifted her hand to push her hair back off her face he noticed a long white scar on the fine blue-veined skin of her wrist. 'How did you get that scar?' he asked.

A mask came down over her features as she pushed down her sleeve. 'I broke my arm when I was a kid. I had to have it pinned and plated.'

Julius let a silence slip past. He watched as she fiddled with the hem of her sleeve, her fingertips tugging and twisting the light cotton fabric as if it irritated her skin. Her eyebrows were drawn together, her forehead pleated, her expression broody. It intrigued him how quickly she had switched from impudent vamp to bad-tempered brat.

'Would you like to look around the villa?'

She gave an indifferent shrug. 'Whatever.'

Julius had intended to get Sophia to give Holly a guided tour but he decided he would do it. He told himself it was so he could check she didn't pilfer any of his belongings or carve her initials or a curse word into one of his antiques. Why on earth had he agreed to this? God knew what she would get up to once out of his sight.

He led the way out of his office. 'I detect a trace of an English accent,' he said as they walked along the hall. 'Are you originally from the UK?'

'Yes,' she said. 'We moved out here when I was young. My father was Argentinian.'

'Was?'

'He died when I was three. I don't remember him, so there's no need to get all soppy and sentimental and feel sorry for me.'

Julius glanced down at her walking beside him. She barely came up to his shoulder. 'Is your mother still alive?'

'No.'

'What happened?'

'She died.'

'How?'

Holly threw him a hardened look. 'Didn't Natalia show you my file?'

Julius was a little ashamed he hadn't read it in more detail. But then he hadn't planned on having anything to do with her. Apart from Sophia, he didn't have much to do with his staff on a personal level. They did their job. He did his. He'd focussed on Holly's rap sheet without looking at the story behind the miscreant behaviour. Some people were born bad, others had bad things happen to them and they turned bad as a result. Where did Holly fit on the spectrum? 'I'd like you to tell me.'

'She killed herself when I was seventeen.'

'I'm sorry.'

She gave another careless shrug. 'So what about your parents?'

'They're both alive and well.' And driving him nuts as usual.

Holly stopped in front of a painting. It was a landscape he'd bought at an auction his sister, Miranda, had given him the heads-up on. Miranda was an art restorer, yet another Ravensdale sibling who had disappointed their parents by not treading the boards.

Holly resumed walking, idly picking up objects he had on display, turning them over in her hands and putting them down again. Julius hoped she wasn't sizing them up for later theft.

'You got any brothers or sisters?' she asked after a long silence.

Julius was finding it a novel experience, meeting someone who knew nothing about his family. Didn't the girl have a smartphone? Internet access? Read newspapers or gossip magazines? 'I have a twin brother and a sister ten years younger.'

She stopped walking to look up at him. 'Are you identical?'

'Yes.'

Her eyes suddenly danced with impish mischief, dimples appearing either side of her mouth, completely transforming her features. 'Ever swapped places with him?'

He put on what his kid sister called his 'I'm too old for all that nonsense' face. 'Not for a very long time.'

'Can your parents tell you apart?'

'They can now but not when we were younger,' he said. Mostly because they hadn't been around enough. Their fame was far more important to them than their family. Not that he was bitter. Much. 'What about you? Do you have any siblings?'

'No.' Her dimpled smile faded and the frown reinstated itself on her forehead as she resumed walking along the corridor. 'There's just me...'

Julius heard something in her tone that suggested a resigned sense of profound aloneness. He hadn't expected to feel sorry for her. He had strong values on what constituted good and bad behaviour. The law was the law. Breaking it just because you'd had a difficult childhood wasn't a good enough excuse, in his opinion. But something about her intrigued him. She was light and dark. Moon shadows and bright sunlight. She reminded him of a complicated puzzle that would need more than one attempt to solve it.

Maybe his housekeeper's mission would prove far more interesting than he'd first thought.

Holly stopped in front of the windows overlooking the formal gardens. 'Do you live here alone?' she asked.

'Apart from my staff, yes, but they have separate quarters. Sophia is the exception. She has a suite on the top floor.'

Holly turned and looked at him with a direct gaze. 'Seems a pretty big place for a single guy.'

'I like my own space.'

'Must cost a ton to keep this place ticking over.'

'I manage.'

'Yeah, well, money and possessions don't impress me,' she said, turning to look at the gardens again.

'What does?'

She swivelled to face him and tilted one of her hips, lowering one shoulder lower than the other so her thin chain-store sweater slipped to reveal the creamy cap of her shoulder. She looked at him through eyes half-shielded by the thick dark fans of her lashes. 'Let's see...' She pursed her full lips in thought before releasing them on a breath of air. 'I'm impressed by a man who knows his way around a woman's body.'

Julius was doing his darnedest not even to think about her luscious little body. Or that full-lipped mouth and the mayhem it could cause if it came too close to his. He had a feeling she was testing him. Testing his motives. Seeing if he was going to exploit her. Had she been exploited before? Was that how she viewed all men? As manipulators and bullies who forced their will on her?

He might be a man who liked his own way but there was no way he would ever describe himself as a bully. He could be arrogant at times—stubborn, even—but he was a firm believer in treating women with respect. Having a shy and reserved much younger sister had instilled in him the importance of men taking a stand against all forms of violence against women and girls.

'That's it?' he said. 'Just whether he can perform?'

'Sure,' she said, eyes gleaming with pertness. 'How a man has sex tells you a lot about them as a person. Whether they're selfish or not. Whether they're uptight or casual.' She tapped two of her fingertips against her mouth in a musing manner. 'Let's take you, for instance.'

Let's not, he thought. 'This theory of yours is imminently fascinating but I think—'

'You're a man who likes to be in control,' she said. 'You like order and predictability. You don't do things on impulse. Your life is planned, timetabled, scheduled to the nth degree. Am I right?'

Julius didn't feel too comfortable at being so rapidly written off as a boring stereotype, as nothing more than a cliché. He liked to think he wasn't *that* predictable. He had nuances; sure he did. Layers to his personality that were there if you took the time to find them. He might spend a lot of time in the land of logic and reason but it didn't mean he couldn't use the right side of his brain. Well…occasionally.

He stepped towards the nearest door. 'This is the library,' he said. 'You're welcome to help yourself to books as long as you don't dog-ear them or leave them outside.'

'See?' She gave a bell-like laugh. 'I was spot-on.'

He gave her a look before he moved to the next door farther down the corridor. 'This is the music room.'

'Let me guess,' she said with another one of her impish smiles. 'You don't mind if I play the piano as long as my fingers aren't sticky or I don't drop crumbs between the keys. Correct?'

Julius found the picture she was painting of him increasingly annoying. What gave her the right to sum him up in such disparaging terms? She made him sound like some sort of house-proud obsessive. 'Do you play an instrument?' he asked.

'No.'

'Would you like to learn?' Music was supposed to tame wild things, wasn't it? He could engage a tutor for her. What was that saying about the devil and idle hands? Piano lessons would at least keep her out of his way.

'What?' she said, the cynical glint back in her gaze. 'You think you can teach me the piano in a month?'

'I have other instruments.'

'I just bet you do.'

He gave her a droll look. 'Flute. Tenor recorder. Saxophone.'

She looked at him, one side of her plump mouth curved in a mocking arc. 'Impressive. Gotta love a man who's good with his mouth *and* his hands.'

Julius put his hands deep in his trouser pockets in case he was tempted to show her just how good he was. Why was she being so damn brazen? Winding him up for what reason? To prove he was as predictable as all the other men she'd dealt with? What did she hope to gain? Would he be just another male trophy for her to gloat over? Another man she had slayed with her sensual allure? He wasn't going to fall for it. He had no time for vacuous game playing. She might think him predictable and a walking, talking cliché but he was not when it came to this. She could flirt and tease and taunt him as much as she wanted but he wasn't going to fall into her honey trap. He might be his father's son by blood, name and looks but he wasn't like him by nature.

'I'll leave Sophia to show you around the rest of the house,' he said, his tone formal, clipped. Dismissive.

Her mischievous gaze danced. 'Aren't you going to show me where I'll be sleeping?'

'I'm not sure where Sophia has put you.'

But I hope to God it's nowhere near me, Julius thought as he turned and strode briskly away.

CHAPTER TWO

HOLLY WATCHED AS Julius Ravensdale made his way down the lengthy and wide corridor with long, purposeful strides. She felt strangely breathless after their encounter. Her pulse was thrumming too hard and too fast. It felt as if something small and scared was scrabbling inside the valves of her heart.

Her reaction to him confounded her. Confused her.

Men didn't usually have that effect on her. Even good-looking ones. And they didn't come much better looking than Julius Ravensdale. She'd been expecting some long-haired, bushy-bearded, shoulder-hunched computer geek and instead had found a man who looked as if he could fill in for a European male model in an aftershave or designer watch advertisement. His tall, broad-shouldered athletic build gave him an air of authority that was compelling. There was something about his looks that rang a faint bell of recognition in her head. Had she seen a picture of him somewhere? Or was his twin famous? Even his name struck a chord of familiarity but she couldn't remember where she'd heard it before.

His thick, wavy dark brown hair was tousled in a mad professor sort of way she found intensely attractive.

He was clean-shaven but with just enough regrowth to confirm he hadn't been holding the door for everyone else while the testosterone was being handed out. She had felt the impact of his male hormones as soon as she'd entered his office. It was like a collision against her flesh. Potent. Powerful. Primal. Making her aware of her body in a way she hadn't been in years. Maybe had never been.

He triggered something in her, something deeply instinctive. Something rebellious. She felt an irresistible desire to dismantle his façade of cool civility. To unpick the lock on the brooding passion she could sense was under lockdown. She wanted to tease out the primitive man behind the aristocratic manners. He was so rigidly controlled with an aloof and haughty air. There was an invisible wall around him warning her not to come close. But what if she did? What if she dared to come so close he wouldn't be able to keep that iron control in place? She gave a secret smile. *Tempting thought.*

Holly couldn't get over his incredible eyes. Dark as navy fringed with thick lashes and strong eyebrows. Intelligent eyes. Observant. Intuitive. He had a straight nose and a jaw that hinted at a streak of stubbornness. He looked like he lived in his head a lot. Thoughts and logic were his currency. Action would come later after due consideration.

If nothing else it would make a change from the men she'd been forced to share quarters with—her low-life stepfather being a perfect case in point.

Maybe this month wouldn't be such a hardship after all. It was exhilarating, winding Julius up. It amused her to see him act all schoolmasterish and stern in the face of her brazen behaviour. She was picky when it came to whom she shared her body with but that didn't mean she couldn't have a bit of fun rattling his chain. He was starchy and formal in that 'stiff upper lip' way the well-born English male was known for. Maybe it would fill in the time to try and loosen him up a bit. Show him a top-notch university degree didn't make him any different from any other man she'd met. Men driven by hormones. Greedy to have their lust slaked with whomever was available. She'd prove to him he had no right to look down his nose at her.

Holly gave a little smile. Yep, this period of house arrest could prove to be the best fun she'd had in years.

The housekeeper appeared at the end of the corridor and came towards Holly with her wrist supported in a brace. It brought back memories of the time her stepfather had snapped her wrist when she'd been eleven and then told her he would kill her or her mother if she told anyone how she'd got injured. She'd had to pretend she'd fallen off her bike. A bike she hadn't even possessed. The plates and screws in her wrist weren't the only scars her stepfather had left her with.

Her issues with authority, her rebellious streak, her distrust of men and her cold sweat nightmares were the hoofmarks of a childhood and adolescence spent at the mercy of a madman. She wouldn't have had to be here doing this ridiculous programme if it hadn't been for the way her stepfather and his bullying lawyer had made it seem as if *she* was the criminal.

'Come this way, Holly,' Sophia said as she led the way to the next floor. 'So, what do you think of the place so far?'

'It's okay, I guess.' Holly didn't see the point in getting too friendly with the natives. Sophia seemed nice enough but it would be a waste of energy striking up a friendship when in a matter of weeks—if not before— she'd be gone.

'I had to twist Señor Ravensdale's arm to agree to having you here,' Sophia said as they came to the first-floor landing. 'It's not that he doesn't want to do his bit for charity. He's incredibly generous and supports lots of causes. He just likes to be left alone to get on with his work.'

'Has he got any lady friends?' Holly asked.

Sophia's expression closed down. 'Señor Ravensdale's privacy is of paramount importance to him.'

'Come on, there must be someone in his life,' Holly said.

Sophia's mouth tightened as if she were physically restraining herself from being indiscreet about her employer. 'I value my job too much to reveal such personal information.'

Holly gave a lip shrug. 'He sounds pretty boring, if you ask me. All work and no play.'

'He's a wonderful employer,' Sophia said. 'And a decent man with honour and sound principles. You're very lucky I was able to talk him into having you stay here. It's not something he would normally do.'

'Lucky me.'

Sophia gave her a warning look. 'I hope you're not going to cause trouble for him.'

Who, me? Holly thought with another private smile. Julius Ravensdale's loyal housekeeper thought he had sound principles, did she? How long before his honourable motives were exposed for what they were? She'd seen the way he'd run his gaze over her. He might be clever and sophisticated but he had the same needs as any man his age. He was healthy and fit and in the prime of his life. Why wouldn't he take advantage of the situation? She wasn't vain but she knew the power she had at her disposal. It was the only power she had. She didn't have money or prestige or a pedigree. She had her body and she knew how to use it.

'How'd you injure your wrist?' Holly asked to fill the silence.

'It's just a bit of tendonitis,' Sophia said. 'I get it now and again. It will settle if I rest up. All part of getting old, I'm afraid.'

Holly followed the housekeeper to the third floor of the villa. The Persian carpet was as thick as velvet, the luxurious décor showing French and Italian influences. Gorgeous artworks decorated the walls, portraits and landscapes of various sizes, and marble busts and statues were positioned along the gallery-wide corridor. Chandeliers hung like crystal fountains above and the wall lights sparkled with the same top-quality glitter.

Holly had never been in such an opulent place. It was like a palace. A showcase of every fine thing a sophisticated and wealthy person could acquire. But there were no personal items scattered about. No family photographs or memorabilia. Not a thing out of place and everything in its place. It looked more like a museum than a home.

'This is your room,' Sophia said, opening a door to a suite a third of the way along the corridor. 'It has its own bathroom and balcony.'

Balcony?

Holly stopped dead. Her heart tripped. Fear sent a shiver through the hairs of her scalp. The silk curtains at the French doors leading onto the balcony billowed with the afternoon breeze like the ball gown of a ghost.

How many times had she been dragged to the rickety balcony of her childhood? Locked out there in all types of weather. Forced to watch helplessly as her mother had been knocked around on the other side of the glass. Holly had learned not to react because when she had it had made her mother suffer all the more. Holly's distress revved up her stepfather so she taught herself not to show it.

But she felt it.

Oh, dear God, she felt it now.

Her chest was tight, heavy. Every breath she took felt like she was trying to lift a bookcase. She couldn't speak. Her throat was closed with a stranglehold of panic.

'It's breath-taking, isn't it?' Sophia said. 'It's only been recently renovated. You can probably still smell the fresh paint.'

A shudder passed through Holly's body like an earthquake. Her legs went cold and then weak as if the ligaments had been severed with the swing of a sword. Beads of perspiration trickled down between her shoulder blades, as warm and as sticky as blood. Her stomach was a crowded fishbowl of nausea. Churning. Rising in a bloated tide to her blocked throat.

'I—I don't need such a big room,' she said. 'Just put me in one of the downstairs rooms. We passed a nice one on the second floor. That blue one back there. That'll do me. I don't need my own balcony.'

'But there are nice views all over the estate and you'll have much more privacy. It's one of the nicest rooms in the—'

'I don't care about the view,' Holly said, stepping back from the door to stand near a marble statue that felt as cold as her body. 'It's not as if I'm an honoured guest, is it? I'm here under sufferance. Your employer's and mine. I just need a bed and a blanket.' Which was far more than she'd had in the not-so-distant past.

'But Señor Ravensdale insisted you—'

'Yeah, yeah, I know—be put as far away from his room as possible,' Holly said, hugging her arms across her body. 'Why? Doesn't he trust himself?'

The housekeeper's mouth pulled tight like the strings of an old-fashioned evening purse. 'Señor Ravensdale is a gentleman.'

'Yeah, well, even gentlemen have hormones.'

Sophia let out a frustrated breath. 'Will you at least look at the suite? You might change your mind once you see how—'

'No.' Holly swung away and went back down the stairs, one flight after another, her feet barely landing long enough on each step before it clipped the next one. She didn't draw breath until she got to the nearest exit. She stopped once out in the sunshine, bending forward, hands on her knees, her lungs all but exploding as she gasped in the warm summer air.

There was no way she was going to sleep in a room with a balcony.

No way.

Julius was standing at his office window when he saw Holly striding off towards the lake past the formal part of the gardens. Was she running away already? Absconding as soon as she saw an opportunity? He was supposed to call her caseworker if there was an issue.

He glanced at his phone and then back at Holly's slight figure as she stopped in front of the lake. If she'd wanted to escape she surely would have gone in the other direction. The wide, deep lake and the thick forest fringing it behind were as good a barrier as any. He watched as she bent down and picked up a pebble and skimmed it across the surface of the water. It skipped several times before sinking, leaving a ring of concentric circles in its wake. There was something poignant and sad about her slim figure standing there alone.

There was a tap on his door. 'Señor? Can I have a word?'

Julius opened the door to Sophia. 'Is everything all right?'

'Holly won't have the room I prepared for her,' Sophia said.

He tilted his mouth in a sardonic arc. 'Not good enough for her?'

'Too big for her.'

He frowned. 'Is that what she said?'

Sophia nodded. 'I made it all nice for her and she won't have it. She stalked off as if I'd told her she'd be sleeping in the stables.'

'Whose idea was it to bring her here again?' he said with mock rancour.

'I'm sure she'll grow on you,' Sophia said. 'She's a spirited little thing, isn't she?'

'Indeed.'

'Will you talk to her?'

'I just spent the last half hour with her.'

'Please?' Sophia, for all that she was close to retirement, had a tendency to look like a pleading three-year-old child when she wanted him to do things her way.

'What do you want me to say to her?'

'Insist she take the room I prepared for her,' Sophia said. 'Otherwise where will I put her? You told me you didn't want her on your floor.'

'All right.' Julius let out a long breath of resignation. 'I'll talk to her. But you'd better get the first aid kit out.'

'Come, now. You wouldn't hurt a fly.'

He gave her a wry look as he shouldered open the door. 'No, but our little guest looks as if she could stick a knife in you and laugh while she's doing it.'

Julius found her still skimming rocks across the surface of the lake. She was damn good at it, too. The most he could get was thirteen skips. Her last one had been fourteen. She must have heard him approach as his feet made plenty of noise on the pebbles at the edge of the lake but she didn't turn around. She kept skimming pebble after pebble with a focussed, almost fierce concentration.

'I believe you have an issue with the accommodation I've provided,' he said.

She threw another pebble but not as a skimmer. It went sailing overhead and landed with a loud *plop* in the centre of the lake. 'I don't need a suite in first class. I belong in steerage,' she said.

'Surely that's up to me to decide?'

She turned and faced him. It unnerved him a little to see she had a stone rather than a pebble clutched in her fist. Her eyes flashed at him. 'What are you trying to do? Conduct your own Pygmalion experiment? Well, guess what, Mr Higgins? I'm no fair lady.'

'No; you're a bad tempered little miss who seems intent on biting the hand that's generously offered to feed you.'

She glowered at him with her chest rising and falling as if she was only just managing to control her fury. 'You didn't offer me anything,' she shot back. 'You don't want me here any more than I want to be here.'

'True, but you're here now and it seems mature and sensible to make the best of the situation.'

Holly turned and flung the stone at the lake but it hit a tree on the left-hand side with a loud thwack. 'How are you going to explain me to your fancy friends or family?' she said.

'I don't feel the necessity to explain myself to anyone.'

'Lucky you.'

Where was the cheeky little flirt now? he wondered. In her place was a woman brooding with anger. Anger so thick he could feel it in the air like the humidity before a violent storm.

Julius picked up a pebble and sent it skimming across the surface of the lake. 'That's a personal best,' he said as he counted fifteen skips. 'Think you can match it?'

She turned and looked at him with a watchful gaze. 'What about your girlfriend? What's she going to say when she hears you've got me living with you?'

He bent down and picked up another pebble, rolling it over to check its suitability. 'I don't have a current girlfriend.'

'When was your last one?'

He glanced at her before he skimmed the pebble. 'You ask a lot of questions, don't you?'

'I know you're not gay because no gay man would look at me the way you did back in your office,' she said. 'You fancy me, don't you?'

Julius tightened his mouth as he reached down for another pebble. 'Your ego is as appalling as your manners.'

She gave a cynical laugh as she threw another pebble, even farther this time, as if all her pent up energy went into the throw. 'I suppose no one without a university degree with honours need apply. So what do you talk about in bed? Quantum physics? Einstein's theory of relativity?'

He looked down at her upturned face with its mocking smile and impossibly cute dimples. What was it about her that made him feel this was all a front? He was all too familiar with theatrical talent. His parents were some of the best in the theatre. Even he had to acknowledge that. But this defiant tearaway was putting on an award-winning performance. 'Why don't you want the room Sophia prepared for you?' he asked.

Her eyes lost their cheeky sparkle and her expression became sulky again. 'I don't want to be shoved at the top of your grand old house like some freak you want to hide in case she does the wrong thing in front of your fancy guests. I suppose you'll insist on me taking my meals in there or with the servants in the kitchen.'

'I don't have servants,' Julius said. 'I have staff. And, yes, they make their own arrangements over dining but that's more out of convenience than convention.' He paused for a beat before adding. 'I expect you to dine with me each evening.' *Are you out of your mind? The less time you spend with her the better.*

'Why?' she said with a surly look. 'So you can criticise me when I use the wrong fork or knife?'

'Why do you think everyone you meet is automatically against you?'

She turned and looked at the lake rather than meet his gaze. He could see the flicker of a tiny muscle in her cheek as if she was grinding down on her molars.

It was a while before she spoke and when she did it was with a voice that was pitched slightly lower than normal with a distinctly husky edge. 'I don't want *that* room.'

'Why not?'

'It's…too posh.'

'Fine,' Julius said, mentally rolling his eyes. 'You can choose your own room. God knows there are plenty to choose from.'

'Thank you.' It was not much more than a whisper of sound and she still wasn't looking at him but there was something in her posture that suggested enormous relief. Her shoulders had lost their tense, bunched-up-to-her-ears look. Her spine was no longer ramrod straight. Her hands were not curled into tight fists or clutching pebbles but hanging loosely by her sides.

He had a strong urge to reach out, take one of her hands and give it a reassuring squeeze but somehow refrained from doing so. Just. 'Do you want to walk back with me or hang around down here for a little bit?' he said.

She turned her head to look at him. 'Aren't you worried I might run away when your back is turned?'

He studied her for a moment, taking in her shuttered gaze and the pouty set to her mouth. 'You'd be running towards prison if you do. Hardly something to look forward to, is it?'

She bit down on her lower lip and turned to look at a water bird that had flown in to land in the centre of the lake, its paddling feet sending out concentric circles of disturbance. He watched as a slight breeze played with some loose tendrils of her hair and she absently brushed them back with one of her hands. His chest gave a sharp little squeeze when he saw her hand was shaking. There was no sign of the tough, angry girl. No sign of the brash guttersnipe. Right then she looked like your average girl next door who had suddenly found herself at an anxiety-inducing crossroads.

Julius bent down, picked up a pebble and handed it to her. 'My brother Jake holds the record down here. Seventeen skips.'

She took the pebble from him but as her fingers touched his he felt an electric shock run up along his arm. She slowly raised her gaze to mesh with his. A pulsing moment passed when he lost all sense of time and place. It could have been seconds or minutes or even days.

His eyes kept tracking to her mouth, the shape of it, the fullness of it that suggested passion and heat, and yet a strange sense of untouched innocence. He felt like a magnet was pulling his head down towards it. He had to fight every muscle and sinew and throbbing cell in his body to counter its force.

He watched as the tip of her tongue slipped out between her lips and moistened the top lip, then the bottom one, leaving each one glistening with a tempting sheen. Blood rushed to his groin, thickening him with a rocket blast of lust.

He had a sudden feeling he had been asleep all of his life until this moment. It was like coming out of cold storage. A slow melt was moving through his body; he could feel it all the way to his fingertips, the urge, the compulsion to touch, to feel her soft skin, sliding, stroking, moving against his own.

His mind was not following its usual logical pathways. It was short-circuiting with erotic images, hot fantasies of him burying himself inside her body, bringing them both to completion in a matter of seconds.

Could she sense the turmoil in him? Had she any idea of the effect she was having on him? He tried to read her expression but her eyelids were lowered over her eyes as she focussed on his mouth.

He lifted his hand to her cheek, barely aware he was doing it until he felt the creamy softness of her skin against his palm, tilting her face so she had to meet his gaze. Those bewitching eyes made his pulse pound all the harder. Every beat of his heart felt like a hammer blow, each one sending a deep, resounding echo to his pelvis. Her skin felt like silk against his palm and fingers. Warm. Smooth. Sensuous. Her eyes contained a glint of anticipation, of expectation. Of triumph.

He moved the pad of his thumb over the small, neat circle of her chin, watching as her pupils flared like pools of ink. Her lips were slightly apart, just enough for him to feel the soft waft of her vanilla-scented breath. How easy would it be to close the distance and touch his lips to hers? The urge to do so was strong, perhaps stronger than at any other time in his life, but he knew if he did it he would be crossing a line. Breaking a boundary. Inviting trouble.

'I'm not going to do it,' he said, dropping his hand from her face.

Her look was all innocence. 'What?'

'You know what.'

She met his eyes with a hard gleam in her own. 'I could make you disregard those principles you're clinging to. I could do it in a heartbeat.'

Julius frowned until his eyebrows met. 'Why are

you trying to ruin your one chance of getting your life in order?'

She glared at him. 'I don't need you to get my life in order. I don't need anyone.'

'How's that been working out for you so far?'

Her eyes were twin flashpoints of heat. 'You know what I hate about men like you? You think just because you have it all, you can have it all.'

'Look,' Julius said. 'I get this is a tough gig for you. You don't want to be here. But what's your alternative?'

She pressed her lips together and looked at him mulishly. 'I'm not the one who should be threatened with going to prison.'

'Yes, well, apparently most prisons are full of innocent people,' he said. 'But according to our current laws you can't steal or damage property or whatever else you did and not be punished for it.'

She swung away. 'I don't have to listen to this.'

'Holly.' Julius caught her by the arm and turned her to face him. 'I want to help you. Can't you see that?'

She gave him a disdainful look as she tested his hold. 'How? By making me get used to all this luxury, only to be tossed back out on the streets as soon as the month is up?'

Julius's frown deepened. 'Don't you have a home to go to?'

Her eyes skittered away from his. 'Let go of my arm.'

He loosened his hold but kept her tethered to him with the bracelet of his fingers. 'No one is going to toss you anywhere,' he said. *What are you going to do with her once the month is up?* The thoughts were like pop-up signs in his head. If she didn't have a home to go to, then where would she go? Where did his responsibility towards her begin and end?

Did he have a responsibility towards her?

'Is that where you've been living?' he asked. 'Out on the streets?'

She slipped her wrist out of his hold and folded her arms across her body, shooting him a fiery glare. 'What would *you* care? People like you don't even notice people like me.'

Julius noticed her all right. A little too much. His hand was tingling where he'd been holding her wrist. It was as if his blood was bubbling through his veins like boiling soda. He noticed the way her brown eyes sparked with venom one minute, glittering with an erotic come-on the next. He noticed the way she moved her body like a sleek pedigree cat, only to turn around, spit and hiss at him like a cornered feral one.

He had no idea how to handle her. He wasn't supposed to *be* the one handling her. This was his housekeeper's mission, not his. He was supposed to be getting on with his work while Sophia did her bit for society by taking in a stray and reforming her.

But Holly Perez was no ordinary stray.

She was a feisty little firebrand who seemed determined to cause trouble with everyone who dared to come too close.

'While you're under my roof I'm responsible for you,' Julius said. 'But that means you have responsibilities, too.'

Her chin came up. 'Like what? Servicing you in the bedroom?'

He set his mouth. 'No. Definitely not.'

Her look said it all. Cynicism on steroids. 'Sure and I believe you.'

'I mean it, Holly,' Julius said. 'I'm not in the habit of bedding young women who have no manners, no respect and no sense of propriety.'

She gave a musical sounding laugh. 'I am *so* going to make you eat your words.'

He stoically ignored the throb of lust that charged through his pelvis. 'I'll see you at dinner,' he said. 'I expect you to dress for the occasion. That means no jeans, no flip-flops and no plunging necklines or bare midriff. Sophia will organise suitable attire if you have none with you.'

Holly gave him a mock salute and a deep, obsequious bow. 'Aye-aye, Captain.'

Julius strode about thirty or so paces before he swung back to look at her but she had already turned back to face the lake. He watched as she hurled a rock as far as she could. It landed in the middle of the water and sank with a loud *plop*, but not before it created tsunami-like ripples over the surface.

CHAPTER THREE

HOLLY WAITED UNTIL Julius was out of sight before she left the lakeside. What right did he have to tell her how to dress? No man was going to tell her what she could and couldn't do. If she wanted to wear jeans, she would wear them. She'd wear high-cut denim shorts and trashy high heels to his stuck-up dinner table if she wanted to. He couldn't force her to dress up like one of his posh girlfriends. He might deny having a current lady friend but no man with his sort of looks went long between hook-ups.

He had *so* been going to kiss her. She had been waiting for him to do it. Silently egging him on. Waiting for him to break. What a triumph it was going to be when he finally did. She would get the biggest kick out of seeing him topple from his high horse. He had no right to lecture her as if she were ten years old. She would show him just how grown up she was. He wasn't dealing with a wilful child. He was dealing with a woman who knew how to make a man weaken at the knees. She would *do* him before he could do her. Although, the thought of having him do her was strangely appealing. He wasn't her type, with his control freak ways, but he was so darn attractive it almost hurt her eyeballs to look at him.

What was it about him that seemed vaguely familiar? His surname kept ringing a faint bell of recognition in her head. Where had she heard the name Ravensdale before?

And then it finally dawned on her.

He was the son—one of the twin sons—of the famous Shakespearean actors Richard Ravensdale and Elisabetta Albertini. They were London theatre royalty; Holly had seen articles about them in gossip magazines. Not that she ever had the money to buy such magazines but occasionally one of the shelters she had stayed in had them lying about.

Julius's parents had married thirty-four years ago after an affair during a London season of *Much Ado About Nothing* and celebrated their first wedding anniversary with the birth of identical twin boys. Seven turbulent years later, they had had a very public and acrimonious divorce. Then, three years later, they'd reunited in a whirlwind of publicity, remarried in a big celebrity-attended wedding service, and exactly nine months later Elisabetta had given birth to a daughter called Miranda.

Holly wondered if Julius had chosen to work and live in Argentina as a way of putting some distance between himself and his famous parents. The attention they attracted would be difficult to deal with, especially since what she had read indicated neither he nor his siblings had any aspirations to be on the stage. He hadn't once mentioned his parents' fame, although he'd had plenty of opportunity to do so.

Was that why he had initially been so reluctant to

have her here? Would her presence draw press attention his way he would rather avoid? If the press got a whiff of her chequered background it might cause all sorts of speculation. Holly could imagine the headlines: *Celebrities' Son Living with Trailer Trash with Criminal Record*. How would that go down with Julius's sense of propriety?

Holly pursed her lips as she thought about her next move. If she called the press it would draw too much attention to herself just now. She didn't want her creep-aholic stepfather to know where she currently was, although, given the friends in high places he had, she wouldn't put it past him to know already or to make it his business to find out.

Franco Morales had influence that had already stretched further and wider than she had planned and prepared for. No sooner would she get herself back on her feet in a new job and a new place than something would go wrong. Her last employer had accused her of stealing from the till. Holly might have a rebellious streak that got her into trouble now and again but she was no thief. But the money had been found in her purse and she'd had no way of explaining how it had got there. Even the shop's security cameras had 'mysteriously' been switched off at the alleged time of the theft.

Holly had been evicted from her last three flats due to property damage that had been wrongfully levelled at her. But she knew her stepfather had staged it, along with the shop theft. He had set her up by sending in a mole to do his dirty work. That was why she had keyed his brand-new sports car and sprayed that message in weed killer on his perfectly manicured front lawn right where his neighbours would see it: *wife beater.*

Holly believed her mother would never have killed herself if it hadn't been for the long years of physical, emotional and financial abuse dished out to her by a man who had insisted on total obedience. Slavish obedience. Demeaning obedience that had left her mother a shadow of her former self. Franco had kept Holly and her mother oscillating between grinding poverty and occasional, large cash hand-outs that he'd never explained where they were sourced from. It was feast or famine. One minute the fridge was full of food. The next it was empty. Or sold. Furniture and appliances would be bought and then they would be sold to solve a 'cash-flow problem'. Things Holly had saved up for and bought with her meagre and hard-earned pocket money would be tossed out in the garbage or disappear without any explanation.

Holly vowed she would *never* break under Franco's tyranny. Even as a young child she had suffered his slaps and back-handers and put-downs without shedding a tear. Not even a whimper had escaped her lips. Not even her 'time-outs' on the balcony had made her give in. Even if her mother hadn't been abused on the other side, Holly would have locked off her feelings; cemented them deep inside. Hardened herself so she could withstand the abuse without giving him the satisfaction of breaking her spirit.

But unfortunately her mother had not been as strong, or maybe it had just become too hard for her to try to protect Holly as well as herself. Holly had never doubted her mother's love for her. Her mother had done everything she could to protect Holly from her stepfather but eventually it had become too much for her. She had become drug- and alcohol-dependent as a way to anaesthetise herself against the prison of her marriage to a beast of a man who had exploited her from the moment he'd met her.

Even though she had only been four at the time, Holly remembered the way Franco Morales had charmed her poor, grieving mother a few months after Holly's father had been killed in a work-place accident. He had taken control of her mother as soon as he'd married her.

At first he had been supportive, taking care of everything so she no longer had to worry about keeping a roof over their heads. He'd even been kind to Holly, buying her toys and sweets. But then things had started to change. He'd begun subjecting her mother to physical and verbal punishment. It had started with the occasional blow-out at first. One-off losses of temper that he would profusely apologise for and then everything would return to normal. Then a week or two would pass and it would happen again. Then it was every week. Then it was every day—twice a day, even.

And then he'd started in on Holly. Insisting she be brought up according to his rules. His regulations. The slaps had begun for supposed disobedience. The backhanders for insolence or often for no reason at all. Holly had got so stressed and wound up by the anticipation of his abuse she would often trigger it so it was out of the way for that day.

Although he'd no longer smacked her once she got a little older, his verbal sprays had worsened as she'd got to her teens. He'd called her filthy names, taunting her with how unattractive she was, how unintelligent she was, how no one would ever want her. All of which had been confirmed when her mother had died. Holly hadn't known what to do, where to go, how to manage her life.

During that awful, anchorless time she had done things she wished she hadn't and not done things she wished she had. She had mixed with the wrong people for the right reasons and mixed with the right people for the wrong reasons.

But things were going to be different now.

Holly was determined to get her life heading in the right direction. Once this community service was over, she was going to go to England, as far away as possible from her stepfather, back to the country of her mother's birth.

Then, and only then, would she be free.

Holly walked back towards the villa via the gardens. There were hectares of them, both formal and informal. There was even a swimming pool set on a sundrenched terrace that overlooked the fields where some glossy-backed horses were grazing. The summer sun was fiercer now than earlier. The clouds had shifted and the bright light sparkled off the swimming pool like thousands of brilliant diamonds scattered over the surface. She bent down and trailed her fingers in the water to test the temperature. It was deliciously, temptingly cool. Not that she was much of a swimmer, but the thought of cooling off was irresistible.

She glanced at the villa to see if anyone was watching. Not that she cared. If she wanted to have a dip in her underwear who was going to stop her? She kicked off her sandals and shimmied out of her jeans, dropping them in a heap by the pool. She hauled her cotton sweater and the vest top she was wearing under it over her head and sent it in the same direction as her jeans.

Holly stood for a moment as the sun's rays soaked

into her all but naked flesh. She pushed all her thoughts about her bleak childhood out of her head. They were like toxic poison if she allowed them to stay with her too long. Instead, she pretended she was on holiday at an exclusive resort where she had total freedom to do what she wanted.

And then, taking a deep breath, she slipped into the water and let it swallow her into its refreshingly cool and cleansing embrace.

Julius heard a splash and pushed his chair back from the computer to check who was using the pool. He should've guessed and he *definitely* shouldn't have looked. Holly was swimming, wearing nothing but what looked like a transparent bikini. Or was it a bikini or just her bra and knickers? He knew he should get away from the window. He even heard the left side of his brain issue the order. But the right side wilfully drank in the sight of her. Lustfully feasted on the vision of her playing like a water sprite. Her lithe limbs and pert breasts with their pink-tipped nipples showing through the thin cotton of her bra tantalised his senses and drove his blood at breakneck speed to his groin. Her wet hair was slicked back and looked as dark as the pelt of a seal. She did a duck dive, and he caught a delicious glimpse of her neat bottom, long legs and thoroughbred-slim ankles. She kicked herself to the bottom of the pool before re-surfacing like a dolphin at play. He heard the sound of her tinkling laughter just as she went back down for another dive.

When she came up she had her back to him. He saw the neat play of the muscles of her back and shoulders as she lifted her hair off her neck, using its length to tie it in a makeshift knot on top of her head. She went back under the surface with a splash of her legs and ballerina-like feet.

The agility of her firm young body drove his stunned senses into overdrive. She could have been a model showcasing a new line of swimwear. She was athletically slim but with just the right amount of curves to make his blood pound with heightened awareness.

He couldn't take his eyes off her. He was mesmerised by the vision of her. The way she moved as if she had no care for whoever might be watching. The way she played like a fun-loving child and yet her body was all sensual woman.

When she came up the next time she turned her body so she was facing his window. As if she had some internal tracking device, her gaze honed in on his office window. She raised one of her brows before her mouth slanted in a knowing smile as she gave him a cheeky little fingertip wave.

Julius let out a stiff curse and turned away. He raked a hand through his hair, hating himself for the way his body reacted to her of its own volition. He had no control over it.

He saw. He ached. He throbbed. He *lusted*.

It shocked him how easily she reduced him to the level of an animal looking for a chance to mate. Surely he had more taste than to have his tongue hanging out for an outrageous tease? How was he going to survive a month of this? With her flaunting herself at every available opportunity? What was she doing, playing in the pool? This wasn't a holiday resort, for God's sake. She was here to work.

And, God damn it, he would make sure she did.

* * *

Holly heard the tread of firm footsteps coming along the flagstones as she sat on the top step of the pool idly kicking her feet just under the water. She stopped kicking and looked over her shoulder to see Julius striding towards her with a brooding expression on his face.

'Having fun, are we?' he said.

'Sure.' She gave him a breezy smile. 'Why don't you join me? You look like you could do with a little cooling off.'

Something dark and glittering flashed in his navy-blue gaze as it collided with hers. 'You're not here on holiday.' His tone was terse. Curt.

Holly felt a little thrill course through her body at the way he was trying not to look at her wet breasts. Her well-worn cheap bra was practically as sheer as cling film. His jaw had a tight clench to it as if his teeth were being ground together like chalk. She could see the tiny in-out movement of a muscle near the side of his flattened mouth. *Go on*, she silently dared him. *Have a good old look.* She arched back against the pool steps so that her breasts were above the water line. She watched as his eyes dipped to her curves, where the water was lapping her erect nipples, before he dragged his gaze back to hers, his mouth a flat line of disapproval.

'I don't see why I shouldn't be allowed to make use of what's on offer,' she said with a sultry smile.

'Get out,' he said with a jerk of his head.

Holly arched one brow at him. 'I would've thought those posh celebrity parents of yours would've taught you better manners than that. Say the magic word.'

He said a word but it had nothing to do with magic. It was a colourful swear word with distinctly sexual connotations that made the atmosphere between them even more electric.

Holly felt an unexpected frisson deep in her core, a flicker of arousal that licked along her flesh like the tail of a soft leather whip. Julius's nostrils were wide, flaring like a stallion about to rear up to take charge of its selected mate. She had never seen a man look so magnificently stirred by her. The sense of power it gave her was tempered only by the fact he stirred her in equal measure. He *aroused* her. He turned her on to the point where she could feel her body contracting with want. It was a new experience for her. She was usually the object of desire while feeling nothing herself. But this was different. She felt urges and cravings that were overpowering to say the least.

'You either get out on your own or I'll get you out,' he said through clenched teeth.

Holly gave a mock shudder. 'Ooh! Do you promise? I love it when a man gets all macho with me.'

His jaw clamped down so hard she heard his back teeth connect. 'Firstly, you're not dressed appropriately,' he said. 'I have staff members about the property—both young and old—who would be offended by your lack of modesty.'

Holly laughed at his priggishness. He wasn't worried about his staff. He was worried about himself. How she made him feel—out of control and unsettled by it. *What fun this was turning out to be.* 'Are you in some sort of time warp?' she said. 'This is the twenty-first century. Women can dress how they want, especially on private property.'

'Secondly, you're not here to party,' he said as if she hadn't spoken. 'You're here to work. W-O-R-K. Maybe you haven't heard that word before. But by the time you leave I swear you'll know it intimately or I'll die trying. Sophia is waiting for you in the kitchen. There's a meal to prepare.'

'Go help her yourself,' she said with playful splash of her toes that sent a spray of water over his crisply ironed trousers. 'You've got two arms.'

Those two strongly muscled arms suddenly reached down into the water and hauled her to her feet to stand dripping in front of him. Close to him. So close she could feel his body heat radiating towards her. Any second now she thought she would hear the hissing of steam.

'I gave you an order,' he said, breathing hard, eyes glittering darkly.

Holly stood her ground even though his hands gripping the tops of her arms were searing through her flesh like scorching-hot brands. The proximity of his hard body was doing strange things to hers. She could feel a pulse of excitement roaring through her flesh, a zinging awareness of all that was different between them: his maleness, her femaleness, his determination to keep control and her determination to dismantle it.

It crackled in the air they shared like a current set on too high a voltage.

She looked at his grimly set mouth and the dark shadow of sexy stubble that surrounded it. The clench of his jaw that suggested he was only just holding on to his temper. Her heart began to thump, but not out of fear. It wasn't him she was afraid of but her reaction to him. She had never felt her body react in this way. His touch triggered something raw and primal in her. She had never felt her body *ache*. Pulse and contract with a longing she couldn't describe because she had never felt it quite like this before. She wasn't a virgin but none of her few sexual encounters had made her flesh sing like this. He hadn't even kissed her and yet she felt as if she was on a knife-edge. Every nerve in her body was standing up and waiting. Anticipating. Wanting. *Hungering.*

But then he suddenly dropped his hands from her arms. The movement was so unexpected she nearly toppled backwards into the pool but somehow managed to regain her balance. She maintained her composure—*just*—with a cool look cast his way. 'One thing you should note,' she said. 'I *don't* take orders. Not from you or from anyone.'

His jaw worked for a moment. She saw the way his eyes went to her heaving chest as if he couldn't stop himself. When his gaze re-engaged with hers it burned with heat as hot as a blacksmith's fire. 'Then you will learn how to do so,' he said with a thread of steel in his voice. 'If I achieve nothing else out of this month, I *will* achieve that. You will do as I say and not question my authority. Not for a moment.'

Holly inched up her chin. 'Game on.'

Julius paced the floor of his office a short time later. How could he have let Holly get under his skin like that? He had gone down there to draw a line with her but she had flipped things so swiftly he had ended up acting like a caveman. He had never felt more like slaking his lust just for the heck of it and to hell with the consequences. His body was still thrumming with the thunderous need she had stirred in him.

Holly was doing her best to break him, to reduce

him to the level of a wild animal. She was taunting him with every trick she had in her repertoire. She was in his house, in his private sanctuary, for the next four weeks. *Four weeks!* How was he going to withstand the assault on his senses?

She was so determined, so devious, so...*distracting.* His flesh still tingled with the aftershocks of touching her. Her skin against his had felt hot. Scorching hot. Blistering. He could still feel the sensation firing through his body. Touching her had unleashed something frighteningly primal in him. It roared through his blood like a wild fire. He had been knocked sideways by the sensation of holding her so close to the throbbing need of his body. It had been all he could do to keep himself from ripping that ridiculous see-through underwear away, driving himself into her and thrusting madly until he exploded.

Was he so sex-deprived that her teasing come-on had reduced him to the behaviour of a wild beast? The temptation of her, the thrill of touching her, of smelling that intoxicating scent of jasmine, musk and something else he couldn't pin down had wiped out the motherboard of his morality like a lightning strike.

What was it about her that caused him to react this way? She was wilful, wild, unpredictable and wanton. Being anywhere near her was like fighting an addiction he hadn't even known he possessed. He wanted her. He ached to have her. He pulsed with the need to feel her surround him with her hot little body. He could feel it rippling through him: lust let loose taking charge of him, demanding, dictating, directing. Dismantling all of his efforts to resist it.

He *would* resist it.

He would resist her.

He was not a hedonist. He wasn't a knuckle-dragging Neanderthal who could only respond to primal urges. He had intellect, discipline and self-control. A moral compass. A conscience.

Julius sat down heavily on his Chesterfield office chair, rotating it from side to side as he gathered his fevered thoughts. What was that crack Holly had made about his celebrity parents? So she knew exactly who he was, did she? Had she known all along or had someone told her? Sophia wouldn't have said anything. He trusted his housekeeper to take a bullet for the sake of his privacy. Had Holly somehow stumbled on his identity? No doubt that was why she was playing her seduction game. She wanted a celebrity trophy to hang on her belt. A show business shag to boast about to her friends. Could there be anything more nauseatingly vacuous?

He was lucky the press left him alone here in Argentina. He was able to walk around without the paparazzi documenting his every move. In England it was different. As a child he had found the intrusion terrifying. As an adult it was nothing less than sickening. Being chased down the street, cameras shoved in his face, when he was coming and going to lectures at university. Hounded while he was trying to go on a date with someone. It had got to the point where he had stopped dating. It wasn't worth the effort.

He was often mistaken for his brother, Jake, and that caused heaps of trouble, the sort of trouble for which he had no time or patience. Jake had no issues with the press. Jake accepted it as part of being related to famous people, but then, he had always been the more outgoing twin. Although Jake had no aspirations to be on the stage, he loved being the centre of attention and used their parents' fame to get what he wanted—a constant stream of beautiful women in and out of his bedroom. Jake didn't mind being compared to their father. He wore it like a badge of honour.

Julius would rather poke a skewer in his eye.

He would *not* have people compare him to his father. It wasn't that he didn't love his father. He loved both of his parents in a hands-off sort of way. He had never been one to wear his emotions on the outside. Even as a child he had never been the sort of person who was comfortable with over-the-top displays of emotion. His parents' loud arguments, their torrid displays of temper and their passionate and very public reunions had always made Julius cringe with embarrassment. He was glad he'd spent most of his childhood and adolescence at boarding school. He had found study an escape from the unpredictability of his home life. He had found the structure, order and strictly timetabled life a natural fit for his personality.

Jake, on the other hand, loved spontaneity. Jake hadn't enjoyed the discipline of school and had always found ways to buck the system. He was like their father in that he lapped up the attention and if it wasn't shining his way he found a way to make it do so.

Julius hated the limelight. He liked to work quietly in the background without the world's eye honed on him. His success as an astrophysicist had drawn far more attention to him than he would have liked but he comforted himself with the fact that he was successful in his own right, that he hadn't used his parents' fame as a way of opening any doors. He took a great deal of satisfaction in his work and, although the hours and the responsibility of heading a software company, along with his regular work came with its own set of problems, he enjoyed the flexibility of working from home, flying in and out as necessary.

The fact that the sanctuary of his home was now occupied by a mischievous hoyden was a state of affairs he would have to address, and soon. How was he supposed to concentrate with her flouncing around his villa?

The way she had challenged him as if fighting a duel. *Game on.* What exactly was she trying to prove? Hadn't she done enough by that little strip show in the pool? She was supposed to be making a new start. Reforming her bad ways. But from the moment she'd arrived she'd been playing him like a puppet master. Tugging on his strings until he was so churned up with lust he couldn't think straight. That was no doubt why she wouldn't accept the room Sophia had prepared for her on the third floor. Of course that room wouldn't suit Miss Bedroom Eyes. It was too far away from his. What did she have in mind? A midnight foray into his suite?

He would *not* allow her to win this. She would *not* get the better of him. She might think he was just like any other man she had lured into her sensual web in the past. She might think he was weak and spineless and driven by hormones—but she would soon find she had underestimated him. Big time.

He was putting an end to this before it got started.

Holly Perez was going straight to jail and he was making damn certain she wasn't collecting two hundred pounds—or anything else of his—on the way past.

CHAPTER FOUR

HOLLY WAS HELPING Sophia by preparing the vegetables for dinner while the housekeeper had a lie-down. Not because Julius had *commanded* her to get to work but because Sophia clearly couldn't do much with her wrist in a restrictive brace. Holly remembered all too well how painful a damaged limb could be. The simplest tasks were a nightmare and if you did too much it could compromise the healing process.

Besides, she quite liked cooking, for all that she'd told Julius she couldn't boil an egg, or words to that effect. She even liked cleaning. The repetitious nature of it was somehow soothing. It had helped her many a time as a child and teenager to put some order into the chaos of her home life. Her mother had got to the point of not being able to cope with the running of the home so Holly had taken it over. From a young age she knew how to cook, clean, tidy cupboards, fold washing and iron. It had also been a way to keep her stepfather from criticising her mother for not doing things properly around the house. If the house was as perfect as Holly could make it then a day or two might pass without a showdown.

What Holly didn't like was being ordered about. *Con-*

trolled. No one was going to command her like a serf. If she chose to do something, then she would do it because it was the decent thing to do, or she wanted to do it, not because someone was trying to lord it over her.

As if Holly had summoned him with her thoughts, Julius came striding into the kitchen. 'I want a word,' he said. 'In my office. Now.'

She blithely continued peeling the potato she was holding. 'I'll be there in ten minutes. I've still got the tomatoes and the courgettes to do.'

He came to the opposite side of the island bench to where she was standing and slammed his hands down on the surface, nailing her with his gaze. 'When I issue you an order, I expect you to obey it immediately.'

Holly held his intensely sapphire gaze with an arch look. 'Why can't you talk to me here?' She lowered her voice to a husky drawl. 'Or are you worried your housekeeper will come in and catch us at it on the kitchen bench?'

His eyes went to her mouth for the briefest moment before flashing back to hers, twin flags of dull red riding high on his cheekbones. 'I want you out of here by morning,' he said. 'I'm withdrawing my support for the scheme. You can find some other fool to take you on or you can go straight to jail where you belong. I don't care.'

'Fine.' Holly put down the peeler, untied the apron Sophia had given her and tossed it on the bench. 'I'll go and pack my things. Sophia can take over here. I'll just go and wake her from her nap and tell her. Her wrist was giving her a lot of discomfort earlier so she took a stronger painkiller. I reckon she's been doing too much because she doesn't want to let you down. But, hey, that's what she's paid for, right?'

He glanced at the half-prepared meal before reconnecting with Holly's gaze. 'You—' he bit out. 'This is one big game to you, isn't it?'

Holly leaned over the bench so her cleavage was on show. He reared back as if the backdraft of a fire had hit him in the face. 'You know what your trouble is, Julius? You don't mind if I call you that, do you? It makes things a little less formal between us since we're living together and all, don't you think?' She heard his teeth audibly grind together as she fluttered her eyelashes at him but she carried on regardless. 'Your problem is you're sexually frustrated. All that pent-up energy's gotta have an outlet. You're tearing strips off me when what you really want to do is tear my clothes off.'

His expression was thunderous. 'I have *never* met a more audaciously wanton woman than you. You have zero shame.'

Holly gave him an impish smile. 'Aw, how sweet of you to say so. Such flattery is music to my ears.'

He muttered a savage swear word and pushed his hair back from his forehead. It looked as if it wasn't the first time he'd done it that evening. The thick, glossy strands were in a rumpled state of disorder. His whole body was taut, rippling with tension. He reminded her of a tightly coiled spring about to snap.

'Here's what you've got wrong about me,' he said, facing her again with a hardened glare. 'I *can* resist you. You might think all those come-on looks will make me fall on you like some hormone-driven teenager, but you're wrong.'

Holly held out her hand, palm up. 'Want to lay a bet on it?'

He eyed her hand as if it were something poisonous. 'I don't gamble.'

She laughed. 'You're even more boring than I thought. What are you afraid of, Julius? Losing money or compromising one of your starchy old principles?'

He gave her a black look. 'At least I have some, unlike some other people I could mention.'

'Like your father?' Holly wasn't sure why she thought immediately of his father. But she'd heard enough about Richard Ravensdale's reputation to wonder how Julius could possibly be his son. Julius was an apple that had rolled so far away from the tree it was in another orchard. He was so uptight and conservative. His brother, Jake, was another story, however. Jake's exploits were plastered over the internet. It made for very entertaining reading.

Julius's brows snapped together in a single black bar. 'What do you know about my father?'

'He's a ladies' man,' Holly said. 'He's what I'd call a triple-D kind of guy: dine them, do them, dump them is his credo, isn't it? A bit like your twin brother's.'

'You didn't let on that you knew who my family was earlier,' he said. 'Why not?'

Holly gave him a cheeky smile. 'Fame doesn't impress me, remember?'

His mouth tightened until his lips almost disappeared. 'This is a bloody nightmare.'

'Hey, I'm not judging you because of your parents,' Holly said as she resumed preparing the vegetables. 'I reckon it would totally suck to have famous parents. You'd never know who your friends were. They might only be hanging out with you because of your connection with celebrity.' She looked up to find Julius staring at her with a frown between his brows. 'What's wrong?'

He gave his head a little shake, walked over to the fridge and opened it to take out a bottle of wine. 'Do you want one?' He held up the bottle and a glass.

'I don't drink.'

His gaze narrowed a fraction. 'Why not?'

Holly shrugged. 'I figure I've got enough vices without adding any more.'

He leaned back against the counter at the back of the kitchen as he poured a glass and took a deep draught of his wine. And another. And another.

Holly shifted her lips from side to side. 'You keep going like that and Sophia won't be the only one around here needing strong painkillers.'

'Tell me about your background,' Julius said suddenly.

Holly washed her hands at the sink. 'I expect it's pretty boring compared to yours.'

'I'd still like to know.'

'Why?'

'Humour me,' he said. 'I'm feeling sorry for myself for having a triple-D dad.'

'Aww. All those silver spoons stuffed in your mouth giving you toothache, are they? My heart bleeds. It really does.'

He screwed up his mouth but it wasn't a smile. More of a musing gesture, as if he were trying to figure her out. 'I know I come from a privileged background,' he said. 'I'm grateful for the opportunities it's afforded me.'

'Are you?' Holly asked with an elevated eyebrow.

His frown carved a V into his forehead. 'Of course I am.'

'So that's why your housekeeper had to twist your arm to do your bit for charity?' she said. 'To convince you to help someone a little less fortunate than yourself? Yeah, I can totally see how grateful you are.'

He had the grace to look a little uncomfortable. 'Okay, so you weren't my first choice as a charity, but I give to other causes. Generously, too.'

'Anyone can sign a cheque,' Holly said. 'It takes guts to get your hands dirty. To actually physically help someone out of the gutter.'

'Is that where you were?'

She challenged him with her gaze. 'What do you think?'

He held her look for another pulsing moment. 'Look, I'm sorry we got off to a bad start. Maybe we could start over.'

'I don't think so,' Holly said. 'You've already made your mind up about me. It's what people like you do. You make snap judgements. You judge people on appearances without taking the time to get to know them.'

'I'm taking the time now,' Julius said. 'Tell me about you.'

'Why should I?'

'Because I'm interested.'

'You're not interested in me as a person,' Holly said as she checked the oven where she had put the galantine of chicken earlier. 'You just want me out of here because I make you feel uncomfortable.'

'That was your intention, wasn't it?'

Holly closed the oven door and faced him. 'You want to know about me? I'm twenty-five years old. I had my first kiss at thirteen and my first sex partner at sixteen. I left school at seventeen without finishing my education. I have no qualifications. I speak two languages, English and Spanish—three, if you count sarcasm. I don't drink. I don't do drugs. I hate controlling men and I have issues with authority. That's about it.'

He glanced at the vegetable dish she had prepared. 'You told me you couldn't cook.'

'So I lied.'

'Why?'

Holly gave a lip-shrug. 'Felt like it.'

He came over to where she was standing. He stopped within touching distance but kept his hands by his sides. Even so, she could feel the magnetic pull of his body against hers. It was like a force field of energy. Strong. Powerful. Irresistible.

She glanced at his mouth, wondering if he was going to lean in to kiss her. She suddenly realised how much she wanted him to. Not to prove her point; somehow that agenda had taken a back seat, so far back it was now in the boot. No, she wanted him to kiss her because she really wanted to know what his mouth felt like. How it would feel as it moved over hers. How it would taste. How his tongue would feel as it stroked along hers. *Mated* with hers.

Then he did touch her. It was a fleeting stroke of two of his fingers down the slope of her cheek in a movement as soft as an artist's sable brush. It sent a shockwave through her senses. Every nerve in her face began tingling, spiralling in dizzy delight. She moistened her lips, barely aware she was doing it until she saw the way his sexily hooded gaze followed the pathway of her tongue.

Holly slowly brought her gaze back up to the midnight-sky-dark intensity of his. His expression was unfathomable. She didn't know what he was thinking. What he was feeling. She was scarcely able to think clearly herself. And as to her feelings… She didn't allow her feelings to get involved when she got physical with a man. *Never.*

'Who are you, Holly Perez, and what do you want?'

'I really should've made you lay down some money,' she said.

'You think I'm going to kiss you?'

'You're thinking about it—that much I *do* know.' *Why am I speaking in such a husky whisper?* Holly thought. Anyone would think she was falling under some sort of crazy spell. Sure, he was handsome and he smelled good. Way too good, compared to some of the men she'd been up close and personal with. But he was a man who wanted to tame her and that she could never allow. Not in a million years.

His mouth tilted in a half smile. 'You think you can read my mind?'

'I don't know about your mind but your body's giving off one heck of a signal,' she said.

'So is yours.'

Tell me something I don't already know, Holly thought, sneaking in a hitching breath. Somehow the power base between them had shifted. She was no longer in charge of her body. It was reacting according to its own schedule, a schedule she had no control over. Her senses were scrambled. Caught up in a maelstrom of feelings she had never encountered before. Desire was running like a hot fever in her blood. She could feel her own wetness between her legs. She wondered if he could smell the musk of her arousal. She could feel the tingling of her breasts in anticipation of him reaching for them. As it was, his chest was barely half an inch away from hers.

In the past her breasts had felt nothing when a man stood close to her. They were just there—part of her anatomy. Now they were deeply sensitive erogenous zones that craved contact. They pushed against the fabric of her bra, swelling in need, her nipples peaking in response to his presence.

She could even sense the swell of his erection close to where her pelvis pulsed with need. The hot, hard, swollen heat of him was sending out a signal like sonar to her body, making her ache and throb with want.

'I would only sleep with you to prove a point,' Holly said in a way she hoped sounded offhand. 'Sorry if that offends your ego.'

He picked up one of her curls and wound it around his index finger. The gentle tug on her scalp sent a shot of lust between her legs, turning her core to molten fire. His eyes were so dark they reminded her of deep outer space. Limitless. Fathomless. 'It doesn't, because we're not going to sleep together.' His voice was only slightly less husky than hers.

'Could've fooled me.'

He pressed the pad of his thumb against her lower lip, holding it there for a moment before lifting it away. But still he didn't move away from her. His body was toe to toe with hers. If she leaned forward a fraction, their thighs would touch. The temptation to do so was like an invisible hand pushing her from behind. She brushed against the unmistakable hardness of him. Felt the shock through her flesh like a powerful current. It shot through her body in an arc of erotic energy that left no part of her unaffected. She saw the way his pupils flared, his eyes darkening, pulsing and glinting with want.

'You want me so bad I bet all it would take is one little kitten-lick of my tongue to send you over the edge,'
Holly said, shocking herself at her wanton goading of
him. Why was she being so utterly brazen? He had the
edge on her here. He had already told her he would evict
her from the programme. That had been his intention
when he'd come down to speak to her. She would be sent
to prison. She had no second chances. If she pushed him
too far, he would get rid of her. Wasn't that what *everyone* did to her? She knew what was at risk but even so
she couldn't stop herself. She was driven by the urges
of her body—her traitorous body—which seemed to
have developed an agenda of its own.

Julius sent a fingertip from the top of her cleavage,
down the length of her sternum, over her quivering belly
and then down to the zip of her jeans. He outlined the
seam of her body through the denim and metal teeth of
her zip, all the while holding her gaze with the smoul-
dering blaze of his own. 'I bet I could make you come
first,' he said in a two-parts gravel, one-part honey tone.

Holly almost came on the spot. She felt the flicker-
ing of her nerve endings, the swelling of her body as it
ached and throbbed for more stimulation. She had to
get away from him before he won this. He had far more
self-control than she had bargained for and certainly
far more than she had. What was he…made of steel?

'I could be faking it and how would you know?'
she said.

His mouth slanted again in a cynical smile. 'I would
know.'

Holly let out a breath that caught at her throat like a
tiny fishhook. 'In my book, sexual confidence in men
is arrogance in disguise.'

He outlined her mouth with that same lazy, tantalising glide of his finger. Tracing, touching, teasing her lips until she wanted to suck his fingertip into her mouth and draw on it as if she was drawing on him intimately. Not that she ever did that. Not for anyone. She hated it. It was gross and so were the men who insisted on it. But something about Julius made her want to step outside her boundaries. He triggered all sorts of forbidden urges in her. Was it because he was so conservative? Or was it because he was the first man she had ever felt this raging, red-hot passion for?

'You think I'm arrogant because I can pleasure you like you've never been pleasured before?' he asked.

'Promises, promises,' Holly said in a singsong voice.

He upped her chin between his finger and thumb so her gaze had nowhere to go but to mesh with his. The burn of his touch moved through her body like a trail of fire. The scorching circle of his thumb beneath her chin sent her pulse into overload.

His eyes moved between hers, back and forth, like the beam of a searchlight. She felt the magnetism of him, the sheer power he had over her with his laserlike touch. The touch she craved in every pore of her body. Her flesh ached to feel his hands move all over her. To shape and caress her breasts, her thighs and what pulsed and fizzed with longing between them. The need was thrumming inside her like the twang of a cello string plucked too hard. It reverberated through her racing blood, tripled her heartbeat and sent her already scudding pulse haywire.

'You're beautiful, but you know that, don't you?' Julius said in a deep, rough baritone that sent another tremor of want through her core. 'You know the power you have over men and you use it every chance you get.'

'A girl's gotta do what a girl's gotta do,' Holly said, trying to keep her gaze from skittering away from his probing one, trying to keep the fragile hold on her equilibrium disguised. Never had she felt such a compulsion to indulge her senses, to lose herself in a feast of the flesh, to allow herself to be consumed by the power and force of attraction and lust.

He threaded his fingers through her hair, lifting it away from her scalp, only to let it fall in a bouncing cascade against her neck and shoulders. 'That's why you were cavorting out in the pool,' he said. 'You wanted my attention. How better to get it than to strip off and parade that beautiful, tempting body beneath my office window?'

'You didn't have to look,' Holly said. 'You could have drawn the curtains or pulled the blind.'

He gave a little sound of sardonic amusement. 'You're not going to pull my strings like I'm some spineless puppet. I'm made of much sterner stuff.'

That goading little devil was back on Holly's shoulder, urging her to push Julius as far as she could. 'So that's why you came stomping out to the pool and manhandled me out of the water, was it? Just to show how stern and disciplined you are? Don't make me laugh.'

His eyes flashed with a flicker of anger. The same beat of anger she could see in a muscle beside his mouth, flicking on and off like a faulty switch.

The tug of war between his gaze and hers went on for endless seconds.

The air bristled with static.

But then he suddenly stepped back from her with

a muttered expletive. Holly hadn't realised she'd been holding her breath until he walked out of the kitchen without a backward glance.

She expelled the banked-up air in a long, jagged stream.

Round one a draw, she thought. *You'll win the next.*

But a nagging doubt tapped her lightly on the shoulder... *Maybe you won't.*

CHAPTER FIVE

JULIUS STRODE OUT of the villa in search of fresh air. Of common sense. *Control*. Where the hell was his control? He was furious with himself for allowing that toffee-eyed little temptress to trigger his hormones. Why hadn't he kept to his plan? He owed her nothing. What did he care if she went to prison? It was where she belonged. Why had he allowed her to manipulate his conscience?

Or maybe it wasn't his conscience she'd manipulated...

He was disgusted with himself for wanting her like he had wanted no other woman. He was annoyed he had allowed her to needle him to the point where he was as close to breaking as never before. How could he have allowed that to happen? He wasn't the sort of man who put sex before sense. This was nothing but a game to her.

She could tease and taunt him all she liked. She could walk around his villa scantily clad. She could flash her delectable cleavage at him. She could wiggle her hips and pert bottom. She could pout her sexy little mouth at him all day long. She could swim in his pool stark naked for all he cared.

He would *not* let her win this.

He had been tricked by her chameleon-like behaviour. The way she'd fooled him by her charitable act of taking over the cooking while Sophia had rested, after she'd been so adamant she wasn't going to take orders from him or anyone.

What was true about her and what were lies?

She was a smart-mouthed, streetwise siren. Flirting with him, teasing him, daring him, goading him until his blood ran so hot and fast through his veins it scorched him. He was burning for her. Throbbing with the ache to have her. He had never felt desire like it. It was like a storm in his body. A powerful combustion of energy that built each time he was near her. It was brooding inside him even now. The pressure of high arousal. The ache of unreleased desire was a burning ache he couldn't tame or dismiss. It consumed his thoughts as well as his flesh. Wicked, damning thoughts of what he would like to do to her—*craved* to do to her.

His brain was racing with a constant loop of hot images of them having sex like jungle animals. No 'finesse' sex. Hard and fast sex. 'Any position' sex.

Holly Perez was the most dangerous woman he had ever met. With her bedroom eyes and wily ways, she threatened everything he stood for. She made him feel things he had trained himself not to feel. Emotions were things he controlled. Desires were something he properly channelled. He did not rush into mad flings and one-nighters with strangers, especially ones with a criminal past.

He had standards. Principles. He was a good citizen who paid his taxes on time. He never coloured outside the lines. Damn it, he didn't even park outside of them.

Call him conservative, or even obsessive, but rules were things he respected because for most of his life his parents had disregarded them. Rules provided structure in a disordered world. He liked order. He liked predictability. Planning was his forte. He didn't do things on the fly. He wasn't spontaneous. He wasn't a risk taker. He left that sort of thing to his brother, Jake, who loved to live life in the fast lane. Julius was only happy in the fast lane if he knew exactly how fast it was, how long, how wide and how long he would have to be in it.

He did the calculations and *then* he acted.

And right now his calculations told him in big neon flashing letters: Holly Perez was danger personified.

But for all that something about her got to him…not just physically, but on an entirely different level. He felt something for her. Something he hadn't expected to feel. He was drawn to her. He couldn't get her out of his mind. He couldn't forget her touch. The way she moved. Even the sound of her laughter—the tinkling-bell sound that made his spine shiver. She was blatant, brazen and in-your-face, yet beguiling. He'd seen a glimpse of vulnerability down at the lake. And when he'd asked her about the scar on her arm. For just a moment he had seen a flicker of something behind the mask she wore. He couldn't help feeling there was more to her than met the eye. Yes, she made him uncomfortable. Yes, she was a flirt. But he had some sort of responsibility towards her, didn't he?

It was only for a month. He would be away for part of that with work. He would hardly have to have contact with her if he chose not to.

And right now the less contact he had with her the better.

Julius was back in his office trying to work when his phone rang. He was in two minds to ignore it when he saw it was his brother calling. 'Jake,' he said heavily.

'Whoa, bro, you sound a little tense there, man,' Jake said. 'So I take it you've already heard the news?'

Julius sat upright in his chair. 'Heard *what* news?'

A list of possibilities went through his head in the nanosecond that followed. His father had had another heart scare. His parents were splitting up. Again. His sister was finally going on a date after losing her childhood sweetheart to cancer when she was sixteen. *No*, he thought; Miranda was too intent on martyrdom. Jake was getting married... *No*. That would *never* happen.

'A skeleton has come out of Dad's closet,' Jake said.

'Another one?' Julius asked, thinking of the veritable cast of mistresses and hook-ups his father had dallied with over the years in spite of 'working at his marriage'. Not that his mother, Elisabetta, could stand in judgement. She'd had a fling or two herself. 'How old is she this time?'

'Twenty-three.'

'God, the same age as Miranda,' Julius said.

'It gets worse,' Jake said.

'Go on, ruin my day,' Julius said.

'She's not his mistress.'

Julius's heart stopped as if a horse had kicked him in the chest. 'He's not a bigamist? Tell me he's not got a secret wife?' *Please, God, spare us all that shame.*

'She's his daughter.'

'His *daughter*?'

'Yep,' Jake said in a grim tone. 'He's sired himself a love child. Katherine Winwood.'

'Dear God, what does Elisabetta think of this?' Julius said. 'How's she taking it?'

'How do you think?' Jake said wryly. 'Hysterically.'

Julius groaned at the thought of the temper tantrums, door slamming and object throwing that would be going on in his parents' hotel suite in New York. He couldn't face another divorce. The last one had been bad enough. The press. The publicity. All of their private lives exposed. 'Is it in the papers?'

'Papers, internet, every social media platform you can poke a finger at,' Jake said. 'It's gone viral. And that's not all.'

Julius's stomach pitched. 'It gets worse?'

'Way worse,' Jake said. 'Kat Winwood was born two months after Miranda.'

Julius did the maths. 'So that means Dad was still seeing this woman's mother when he reconciled with Mum?'

'Got it in one.'

Julius let out a colourful curse. 'What's Dad got to say for himself? Or is he denying it?'

'You can't deny the results of a paternity test.'

'How did this Kat girl get one done?' Julius said. 'Who is she? Where did she come from? Why's she revealed herself now? Why didn't her mother tell Dad she was pregnant, or has he always known?'

'He knew all right,' Jake said. 'He paid the woman to have an abortion. Handsomely, too.'

Julius swallowed a mouthful of bile. Just when he thought his father couldn't shock him any more, he raised it to a whole new level of indecency. 'But she didn't go through with it,' he said unnecessarily.

'Nope,' Jake said. 'She had the kid and kept the father's identity a secret. Even the birth certificate says "father unknown".'

'So why come forward now?' Julius asked.

'She died recently of a terminal illness,' Jake said. 'She told Kat on her death bed who her father was.'

'So this girl Kat is after money.'

'What else?'

Julius scored a hand through his hair. 'How many more like her could there be out there? Why can't Dad keep it in his trousers? He's nudging seventy, for God's sake.'

'I just thought I'd give you the heads up on it in case the press come sniffing around you for an exclusive,' Jake said. 'They've been parked outside my place since the first Tweet went out.'

His brother's words sent an army of invisible ants across Julius's scalp. A drumbeat of panic started up in his chest. His blood ran hot and cold. He felt beads of sweat break out across his brow. If the press came here they would find Holly—*living with him.* A girl not much older than his father's love child. In fact, Holly looked younger than twenty-five. What would the press make of her holed up here with him? Especially if they caught a glimpse of her flaunting her flesh at every available opportunity. They wouldn't wait for the truth. They would jump to sensational conclusions to razz up a storm of scandal.

He had to keep her away from the press. God knew what she would say to them to stir up trouble for him. One look at her and they would assume he was indulging in a lust fest and was no different from his Lothario father. With her sexy little body and her cheeky personality, why wouldn't they assume he was making

the most of the situation? Why, oh, why, had he agreed
to have her here? It was a disaster of monumental pro-
portions.

'You okay, bro?' Jake cut through Julius's racing
thoughts. 'I know it's a shock but think how Miranda's
taking it.'

That was enough to snap Julius back into protective
big-brother mode. 'How *is* she taking it?'

'I haven't spoken to her yet,' Jake said. 'She wasn't
answering her phone. Probably switched it off to keep
the press off her back. But think about it. She's always
been the baby of the family. How's it going to feel to
know there's a new half-sister who's now the youngest?'

'I'll call her as soon as I finish with you,' Julius said,
expelling a long ragged breath. 'Poor kid. You know
how embarrassed she gets by Mum and Dad's behaviour. This will be hardest on her. We've already been
through one divorce with them so we know what we're
in for. She has no idea of how ugly this could get.'

'Yeah, tell me about it,' Jake said. 'But it might not
come to that.'

'You seriously think Mum won't want a divorce after
Dad produces a secret love child out of the woodwork?'
Julius said. 'Come on, Jake. This is our mother we're
talking about. Any chance for a scene and she's right
there in full costume and make-up.'

'I know, but Flynn's trying to smooth things over,'
Jake said. 'Another divorce will be costly to both of
them, and not just financially. Their popularity could
rise or fall according to how they handle this scandal.
You know how fickle the fans are. Flynn's hoping he
can silence the girl with a one-off payment. Something

big enough to keep her mouth shut and go away. Preferably both.'

Julius was relieved to hear it was all in good hands. Flynn Carlyon was the family lawyer; he'd been a year ahead of them at school. He handled Julius's parents' legal affairs as well as run offices in London. Flynn wasn't just a solicitor to the stars. He had won several high-profile property settlement cases that had given him the tagline around the courts: *Flynn equals win.* He had a sharp mind, an even sharper tongue and a cutting wit.

'Have you met this girl?' Julius asked.

'Not yet,' Jake said. 'You might want to drop by next time you're in town and say hello. After all, she's your new baby sister.'

How could I possibly forget? Julius thought with a despairing groan.

Holly put the finishing touches to dinner before she went up to her room on the second floor to have a shower. The room she had chosen was four doors down from Julius's suite but on the opposite side of the wide corridor. It didn't have a balcony—*thank God*—but it did have a nice view over the front gardens and the tree-lined driveway. It had its own en suite, which was decorated in a Parisian style with lovely ceramic-and-brass tap handles and a claw-footed bath that was centred in the middle of the floor, with a telephone-handle fitting as well as taps. There was a separate shower stall big enough for a football team and lots of gorgeous, fluffy white towels, fragrant French soaps and expensive hair products. A gilt-framed oval mirror hung over the pedestal washbasin and there was another full-length one in the bedroom.

The only issue Holly had was with her clothes. They didn't feel right for her surroundings. All this high-end luxury made the clothes she'd brought with her look even dowdier than usual. She had never been financially stable enough to follow fashion. Fashion was something other people followed. Shopping was a pastime other people indulged in. Rich people, people who had money, security and the safety net of family. Holly had taught herself not to want things she could never afford. She had deadened her desire for nice feminine things. It was pointless to wish she could dress like the women she saw about town. Smart women; educated, sophisticated, polished and poised, with hair, make-up and nails done like models and movie stars. She could never compete with that. It was so far out of her reach, she didn't bother trying.

But right now she would have loved a nice dress to put on and some high heels to go with it. Some classy underwear—not cheap, faded cotton but some slinky, cobwebby lace. She would have liked some make-up—not much, just enough to highlight her features, to put some colour on her eyelids and some tinted gloss on her lips. She would have liked to get a decent haircut, perhaps get some professional foils done to cover the pink streaks she'd done with a home kit that hadn't turned out quite the way she'd planned. Maybe a bit of jewellery—pearls, perhaps—to give her a touch of elegance.

But what was the point of wishing she could dress like a glamour girl when all her life she had been the girl with the charity shop clothes? The girl with the bad haircut, the bitten nails and the cheap shoes with the soles worn through? She had always felt like a donkey showing up at a posh dressage event.

Why should now be any different?

After her shower Holly slipped off her towel in front of the mirror. At least she had a good figure. It was her only asset. Good bones; long, slim limbs; a neat waist; nicely shaped breasts; mostly clear skin, apart from that ridiculously childish patch of freckles over the bridge of her nose.

Her gaze went to a pattern of damson-coloured marks around the tops of her arms. She reached up and touched them, her stomach doing a funny little dip and dive when she realised what they were. Julius's fingerprints had branded her flesh with light but unmistakable bruises.

She bit her lip, looking at the grey cotton tank top she had been planning to wear with another pair of jeans—her only pair without holes in them, although they did have a frayed hem. She put on the tank top and picked up a green cardigan, even though the evening was warm, and slipped it on. It wasn't the nicest weave—the acrylic in it always made her skin feel itchy. But it was either that or a denim jacket or a pilled woollen sweater that would have her sweating within seconds. Finally, she bunched up her hair and secured it with an elastic tie in a makeshift knot at the back of her head.

Holly drew in a breath and let it out in a long, slow sigh. Why she was trying to look half-decent for Julius Ravensdale wasn't something she wanted to examine too closely. It wouldn't matter if she'd been dressed in the finest designer wear; he would still look down his imperious nose at her.

Just like everyone else.

CHAPTER SIX

JULIUS HADN'T BEEN able to track down Miranda or his father. But he had fielded several calls from his mother, who was beyond hysterical. He did what he always did. He listened, he stayed calm, he bit his tongue. His mother vented, raged and fumed so much that he began to wonder if she was actually enjoying herself. It was an opportunity to play the victim, one of her favourite roles. His parents' relationship was toxic. He hated the way they were madly in love one minute then hated each other the next. When one did something out of line, the other went into payback mode. It was childish and puerile.

The press was having a ball with this latest bombshell. He'd clicked on a couple of links Jake had sent him. The girl in question was stunning. If her mother had looked anything like Katherine Winwood, Julius could see why his father's head had been turned. Julius only hoped no one would track him down for a comment. His life here in Argentina was his way of flying under the radar. Over here hardly anyone knew who he was and he wanted it to stay that way. But what was he going to do if the press came sniffing around? Holly was a loose cannon. There was a possibility she would deliberately mislead the press if given half a chance. Should he send her away? He looked at his phone. He had the number of her caseworker on speed dial. His finger hovered over it…but then he pushed his phone away.

For all her feistiness and brazen behaviour, there was something about Holly that mystified him. She seemed so determined to challenge him, yet he had seen that glimpse of touching vulnerability down at the lake. He had never met anyone quite like her before. He found her…interesting. Stimulating, and not just because of his overactive hormones. There was a hint of the lost waif about her. Or was he completely hoodwinked by her? Was it his rescue complex in overdrive? He wasn't the sort of person to walk away from a person in need. Holly was difficult and disruptive but if he sent her away now she would have no choice but to go into detention. He knew enough about the penal system to know it was not the place he would want anyone under his care and protection to go. Sophia had been so keen to take Holly on. He would be letting her down if he quit now. The least he could do was talk to Sophia about it. Get her perspective on things.

It was Julius's routine to go to the sitting room before dinner each evening to have a quiet drink with Sophia before she served the meal. It was a pattern they had fallen into over the past few months. He enjoyed hearing about Sophia's extended family and her interesting childhood as the daughter of Italian immigrants. They often spoke in Italian, as he was fluent, given his mother was from Florence.

He wanted to use this time to inform her of his father's latest peccadillo so she could put steps in place to maintain Julius's privacy.

His parents—most particularly his mother—would be appalled at Julius for being so familiar with his housekeeper or, indeed, any of his staff. When he'd been growing up, his parents' housekeeping staff had not been considered part of the family. There'd been strict codes of behaviour forbidding anything but the strictest formality from the staff towards family members. One did not discuss one's private affairs with the staff. One did not fraternise with or consider them as friends. They were employees. They were kept at arm's length. They were taught to know their place and never stray from the boundaries of it.

The only exception had been Jasmine Connolly, the daughter of Hugh Connolly, the gardener at the family property in Buckinghamshire called Ravensdene. Jasmine had come to live with her father after her mother had dropped her at Ravensdene on a visit and was never seen or heard from again. Julius's parents had taken pity on Hugh Connolly—unusual for them, considering their almost pathological self-centredness—and had offered to pay for Jasmine's education. Jasmine was like a surrogate sister to Julius, and certainly to Miranda, as they were much the same age.

Jake, however, had a tricky relationship with Jasmine after an incident when she'd been sixteen. Both blamed the other and as a result they were sworn enemies, which made for some rather interesting dynamics at family gatherings.

But this time it wasn't Sophia who joined Julius for a drink. In walked Holly, carrying a tray with savouries on it, which she put down on the table in front of him, but not before he got a tantalising glimpse of her cleavage as she leaned over.

'Sophia sends her apologies,' Holly said. 'She's having an early night.'

Julius frowned. 'Is she all right? I haven't seen her all day.'

'She's fine. Just needs a rest, is all.'

He watched as Holly poured him a glass of white wine. Clearly Sophia had filled her in on his preferences. She handed it to him with a tight-lipped smile. 'Two standard drinks is all I'll serve. Just so you know.'

He took the glass, only just restraining himself from draining it dry. Mixing one glass of wine with Holly Perez was like drinking five tequilas and expecting to remain sober. It was impossible to remain sober and sensible in her company. He could already feel the tightening of his groin; the stirring of lust her presence triggered was like someone flicking a switch inside him.

For all that he'd wanted to get rid of her, she had turned things around with her concern for Sophia. But was it concern...or conniving behaviour to serve her own ends? He wanted to know more about her. He wanted to know why she was so determined to make trouble for him. It didn't add up. If she made too much trouble, she would be sent to jail. Why then sabotage her last chance at making something of her life? She seemed intent on destroying any hope of a positive future. If he sent in a bad report to her caseworker, it would be disastrous for her. She knew that. He knew that. Why then was she so determined to ruin everything for herself? It didn't make sense. It wasn't logical.

If there was one thing in life Julius demanded, it was sense and logic.

'I thought I told you not to wear jeans to dinner,' he said.

A flash of defiance—or was it pride?—sparked in her caramel-brown gaze. 'I don't have any dresses. I could've come in shorts or my underwear. I can go upstairs and change or I could strip off here. You choose. I'm easy.'

'Undoubtedly.'

She gave him a withering look. 'Not as easy as your old man, according to the news I heard just now.' She sat on the edge of the sofa opposite him. 'He's quite a cad, isn't he? Nothing like you, or so you say.'

Julius forcibly had to relax his hold on the stem of his glass in case he snapped it. 'I would appreciate it if you would refrain from discussing my father's affairs with anyone. If you say one word to the press, I'll send you packing so fast you won't know what hit you.'

'Are you going to fly home to England to meet your new sister?'

He tightened his jaw. 'I'm not planning to.'

'It's not her fault your old man's her father,' Holly said. 'You shouldn't judge her for something she had no control over.'

Julius took another mouthful of wine. She was right and he wanted to hate her for pointing it out to him. But he needed time to get used to the idea of having a half-sibling. He thought he was used to his father's scandals but this one took the prize. The press had been still banging on about it last time he'd looked. Katherine Winwood might be gorgeous to look at but who knew what her motives were in coming forward? Money, most probably. That she might be entitled to some compensation for how his father had treated her mother was not something he wanted to comment on. He was sick to the stomach over his family's dramas. What or who would turn up next?

Julius decided a change of subject was called for. 'I'll order some clothes for you. Let me know your size and I'll make sure you have what you need.'

Holly's eyes danced. 'So you're going to be like a sugar daddy to me or something?'

He ground his teeth until his jaw ached. 'No.'

She picked up a canapé and bit into it. 'Pity.'

'It's rude to speak with your mouth full.'

'I'll make sure I remember that when we're in the bedroom,' she said with a naughty smile.

Julius kept his gaze locked on hers but he wondered if she could sense the fireball of lust that hit him. He was suddenly so erect he could feel it pressing against his trouser zip. The thought of her hot little mouth on him made his blood pound in excitement.

He distracted himself by leaning forward to take one of the canapés off the platter. 'Where did you learn to cook?'

'Picked it up along the way.'

He sat back and crossed his right ankle over his left thigh in the most casual and relaxed pose he could manage while his erection still throbbed. Painfully. 'Along the way where?'

'Here and there and everywhere.'

It seemed he wasn't the only one keen to avoid discussing family issues, Julius thought. 'What are your plans once you leave here?'

She gave a loose little shrug before taking another appetiser. 'I want to get a job and save up enough money to go to England.'

'To holiday?'

'To live.' She took a noisy bite and munched away, like a bunny rabbit chewing a crunchy carrot.

Julius knew she was doing it to annoy him. Her rebellious streak was kind of cute, when he thought about it. It reminded him a bit of Jasmine Connolly, the gardener's daughter, who liked to have a bit of fun at times—mostly with Jake, who for some reason didn't see the funny side.

Cute?

What was he thinking? Holly wasn't cute. She was as cunning as a vixen. She was out to prove he was unable to resist her. He was out to prove he could. He had the edge on her. She might be doing all she could to get thrown out of his house but without him as her guardian she would find herself doing time. Why then was she pushing him to evict her? Was it deliberate or a knee-jerk thing? Was her behaviour a pattern she had developed in order to survive? From the scant details she'd given him, her childhood clearly hadn't been a picnic. Did she push people away before they pushed her?

And why did *he* give a damn?

'Do you have relatives in England?' Julius asked.

'My mum was an orphan. My dad was, too. An English couple adopted him, which is how he met my mum over there. It's why they hit it off so well. They were two lonely people who found true love.' Her mouth took a sudden downturn and she looked at the remaining piece of her canapé as if it had personally offended her. 'Pity they didn't get the happy ending they deserved.'

'How did your father die?'

'He was killed in an accident at work.'

'What sort of accident?' Julius pressed a little further.

'A fatal one.'

He gave her a look. 'I realise it's probably painful to talk about but I—'

'It happened a long time ago,' Holly said, interrupting. 'Anyway, I only remember what I've been told.'

'What were you told?'

'That he died in a work-place accident.'

She was a stubborn little thing, Julius thought. She would only reveal what she wanted to reveal. 'Did your mother ever remarry?'

Holly got up abruptly from the corner of the sofa and dusted her fingers on the front of her jeans. 'You want to make your way to the dining room? I'll only be a minute or two. I promised I'd take Sophia's meal up to her.'

Julius sat back and sipped his wine, a thoughtful frown pulling at his brow. So it wasn't his imagination after all. There was definitely something about Holly's background that made her reluctant to speak of it. Could he get her to trust him enough to reveal it?

He pulled himself up short. Why on earth was he even *trying* to understand her?

He was supposed to be keeping his distance. He wasn't the type of guy to let his emotions get the better of him. It was fine to care about her welfare—perfectly fine. Any decent person would do that. But if he thought *too* much about her cute dimples, and pert manner and that far away look she sometimes got in her eyes when she didn't know he was looking, he would be feeling stuff he had no right to be feeling. It was bad enough being attracted to her physically. God forbid he should start liking her as a person. Feeling affection. Holly was a temporary inconvenience and he couldn't wait to get rid of her so he could get his life back into its neat, ordered groove.

Even if at times—he reluctantly conceded—it was a little boring.

* * *

Holly made sure Sophia was settled in her suite with her meal, a drink and the television remote handy. She had cut up the chicken and the vegetables so Sophia could eat with her left hand using a fork. 'I'll be back in half an hour to bring up dessert and to clear your dishes,' she said.

'Muchas gracias,' Sophia said with a soft smile. 'You're a good girl.'

Holly gave a little grunt of a laugh. 'Try telling your boss that.'

Sophia looked at her thoughtfully for a moment. 'You don't need to be bad to be noticed. There are other ways to get his attention.'

Holly frowned. 'I'm not trying to get anyone's attention.'

Sophia gave her a sage look. 'Earning someone's respect takes time. It also takes honesty.'

Holly fiddled with a loose button on her cardigan. 'Why should I bother trying to earn someone's respect when I'm not going to be here long enough to reap the benefits?'

'Señor Ravensdale could help you get on your feet,' Sophia said. 'He could give you a good reference. Find employment for you. Recommend you to someone.'

Holly snorted. 'Recommend me for what? Scrubbing someone's dirty floors? No thanks.'

Sophia released a sigh. 'Do you think someone who's in charge of maintaining the upkeep of a house is not worthy of respect? If so, then you're not the person I thought you were. People are people. Jobs are jobs. Some people get the good ones, others the bad ones—sometimes because of luck, other times because of opportunity. But as long as each person is doing the best job they can where they can, then what's the difference between being a CEO and a cleaner?'

'Money. Status. Power.'

'Money will buy you nice things but it won't make you happy.'

'I'd at least like the chance to test that theory,' Holly said.

Sophia shook her head at her. 'You're young and angry at the world. You want to hit out at anyone who dares to come close in case they let you down. Not everyone will do that, *querida*. There are some people you can trust with your love.'

Holly swallowed a golf ball-sized lump of sudden emotion. Her father had called her *querida*. She still remembered his smiling face as he'd reached for her and held her high up in his arms, swinging her around until she got dizzy. His eyes had been full of love for her and for her mother. They had been a happy family, not wealthy by any means, but secure and happy.

But then he had died and everything had changed.

It was as though that life had happened to another person. Holly *felt* like a different person. She was no longer that sweet, contented child who embraced love and gave it unquestioningly in return. She was a hardened cynic who knew how to live on her wits and by the use of her sharp tongue. She didn't feel love for anyone.

And she was darn certain no one felt it for her.

'I'd better go serve His High and Mightiness his dinner,' Holly said. 'I'll see you later.'

'Holly?'

She stopped at the door to look back at the housekeeper. 'What?'

'Don't make things worse for him by speaking to the press if they come here. He doesn't deserve that. He's trying to help you, in his way. Don't bite the hand that's reached out to help you.'

'Okay, okay, already. I won't speak to the press,' Holly said. 'Why would I want to? They'll only twist things and make me look bad.'

'Can I trust you?'

'Yes.'

'He won't let you win, you know.'

Holly kept her expression innocent. 'Win what?'

Sophia gave her a knowing look. 'I know what you're trying to do but it won't work. Not with him. If he wants to get involved with you then it will be on his terms, not yours. He won't be manipulated or tricked into it.'

'That's quite some pedestal you've got him on,' Holly said. 'But then, he pays you good money. You'd say anything to keep your job.'

'He's a good man,' Sophia said. 'And deep down I know you're a good woman.'

You don't know me, Holly thought as she closed the door. *No one does.*

I won't let them.

CHAPTER SEVEN

JULIUS WAS STANDING at the windows of the dining room when Holly came in with the food. She unloaded the tray on the table and then turned briskly to leave.

'Aren't you joining me?' he asked.

Her chin came up. 'Apparently I'm not dressed for the occasion.'

There was a bite to her tone that made him wonder if he had upset her. Embarrassed her. Hurt her, even. She always acted so defiant and in-your-face feisty that to hear that slightly wounded note to her voice faintly disturbed him. There was so much about her that intrigued him. The more time he spent with her, the more he wanted to uncover her secrets. The secrets he caught a glimpse of in her eyes. The shifting shadows on her face he witnessed when she didn't think he was looking at her.

She was an enigma. A mystery he wanted to solve. She played the bad girl so well, yet he saw elements to her that showed her vulnerability, her kindness. Like the way she had taken over the kitchen so Sophia could rest. That showed sensitivity and kindness, didn't it? Or was he being the biggest sucker out to fall for it? Was it all an act? A charade? How could she be as bad as she made out? What was her motive to make him think she was out to seduce him? Was it because he wasn't taking her up on it? Did his refusal to succumb to the temptation she offered make her see him as even more of a challenge?

'It's not a formal dinner,' Julius said. 'If I had guests, then, yes, I would insist on you dressing appropriately. I'm sorry I didn't realise you haven't the suitable attire in which to do so but that will be rectified as soon as possible tomorrow.'

Her small, neat chin came up. 'Once you've coughed up that dictionary you've swallowed, maybe you'll have room for the dinner I've prepared. *Bon appetit.*'

He let out an exasperated breath. 'Look, if I've upset you I'm sorry. But things are a little crazy for me just now.'

Her eyes flashed with unbridled disdain. 'Why would I be upset by someone like you? I don't care about your opinion of me or my clothes. It means nothing to me. *You* mean nothing to me.'

Julius pulled out the chair to the left of his. 'Please join me for dinner.'

Her mouth took on a mutinous pout. 'Why? So you can train me like a pet monkey?' She put her hands on her hips, deepened her voice and did a surprisingly credible imitation of his British accent. 'Don't hold your knife like a dagger. That's the wrong fork. Don't cut your bread. Break it. No, don't call it a serviette, call it a napkin.'

Julius couldn't stop his mouth from twitching. She had definitely missed her calling. She could tread the boards as well as anyone. 'I promise not to criticise you.'

She narrowed her gaze in scepticism. 'Promise?'

He didn't know which Holly he preferred—the snarky challenger or the hot little seductress. Both, he realised with a jolt of surprise, were vastly entertaining. 'Promise.'

She made a little huffing noise. 'Fine.'

He seated her then came around to his own chair and took his place. He spread his napkin out across his lap and watched as Holly expertly served the vegetable dish with silver-service expertise. Then she served the herbed chicken galantine with the same level of competence. She sent him a look from beneath half-mast lashes that made him realise how much he had underestimated her. How much he had misjudged her. She might come across as a bad girl from the wrong side of the tracks but underneath that don't-mess-with-me attitude was a young woman with surprising dignity and class. And pride.

During the course of their meal he made desultory conversation: stuff about the weather, movies and the state of the economy but she didn't seem inclined to talk. The questions he asked her were greeted with monosyllabic responses. He tried using open-ended questions but she just shrugged in a bored manner and mumbled something noncommittal in reply. She didn't eat much, either. She just moved the food around her plate, only taking the occasional mouthful. Was she doing it to punish him? To make him regret his all-too-quick summation of her character and seeming lack of abilities? She was more than capable of holding her own in sophisticated company. Why had she let him believe otherwise? Or was she just contrary for the heck of it? Thumbing her nose up at anyone who judged her without getting to know her?

'Are you not feeling well?' Julius asked.

'I'm fine.'

He studied her for a beat or two. 'You're sweating.'

She gave him a haughty look. 'Ladies don't sweat. They perspire.'

He felt another smile tug at his mouth at the way she so expertly parodied his accent. 'Take off your cardigan if you're hot.'

Her eyes skittered away from his. 'I'm not hot.'

He watched as she made another attempt at her meal but every now and again she would shift in her seat or wriggle her neck and shoulders as if her clothing was making her itchy.

'Holly.'

'What?'

'Take it off. You're clearly uncomfortable.'

'I'm not.'

'Would you like me to adjust the air-conditioning?'

'I told you, I'm fine.'

He shook his head at her in disbelief. 'This afternoon you were parading around half-naked and now you're acting like a nun. What is it with you? Take it off, for God's sake, or I'll take it off for you.'

Her eyes were narrowed as thin as twin hairpins. 'You wouldn't dare.'

'Wouldn't I?'

She shot up from the table and spun around to leave but Julius was too quick and intercepted her. He caught her by the back of her cardigan but when she pulled away from him it peeled off her like sloughed skin.

His heart came to a scudding stop when he saw what was on her upper arms before her hands tried to cover it. The cardigan he was holding slipped out of his hand

and fell to the floor. His mouth went completely dry. His stomach dropped as if it had been booted from the top of a skyscraper.

'Did *I* do that?' His voice came out rusty, shocked. He was ashamed. Mortified.

'It's nothing. I can't even feel it.'

His stomach churned in disgust. 'I hurt you.'

'I bruise easily, that's all.'

Julius scraped a distracted hand through his hair. Dragged the same hand over his face. How could he have *done* this? How could he have been so...so *brutish* to mark her flesh? For what? To prove a point? What point was worth proving if a woman was hurt in the process? It was against everything he believed in. It was against everything that defined him as a man—as a civilised human being. Real men did not use violence. It was the lowest of the low to inflict physical hurt on another person, particularly a woman or a child. How could he have lost control of his emotions to such a point that he would do something like that? He had grabbed her on impulse. He had been so het up about her goading behaviour it had overridden all that was decent and respectful in him.

'Don't make excuses for me,' he said. 'I'm appalled I did that to you. I can only say I'm deeply, unreservedly sorry and assure you it will never, *ever* happen again.'

'Apology accepted.' Her chin came up again, her gaze as hard and brittle as shellac. 'Now, may I get on with serving the rest of the meal?'

Julius had never felt less like eating. His stomach was a roiling pit of anguish. Shame and self-loathing were curdling the contents like acid. He'd thought his father's scandal was bad. This was even worse. *He* was worse.

His behaviour was reprehensible. He had hurt Holly like a thug. 'I think I'll give dessert a miss. Thanks all the same.'

'Fine.' She made a move towards the table. 'I'll just clear these plates.'

'No. Let me,' he said, but stopped short of putting a hand on her arm to stop her. He curled his fingers into his palms. Put his hands stiffly by his sides. 'You see to Sophia. I'll clear away.'

Her eyebrows rose ever so slightly as if she found the thought of him doing anything remotely domestic in nature totally incongruous to her opinion of his personality and station. 'As you wish.'

Julius bent down, picked up her cardigan from the floor and handed it to her. 'I'm sorry.'

'So you said.'

'Do you believe me?' It was so terribly important she believed him. He could think of nothing more important. He couldn't bear it if she didn't believe him—if she didn't trust him. If she didn't feel safe with him. Sure, they could flirt and banter with each other, try to outwit each other with smart come-backs, but there was no way he could bear it if she didn't feel physically safe under his roof—under his protection.

She held his gaze for a long beat, searching his features as if peeling back the skin to the heart of the man he was inside.

'Yes,' she said at last. 'I do. You don't strike me as the sort of man to take his frustration out on a woman.'

'You have experience of those who do?'

Her eyes fell away from his to focus on his top shirt button. 'None I care to recall in any detail.'

Julius wanted to push her chin up so she had to meet

his gaze but he was wary of touching her. He *longed* to touch her. To *hold* her. To reassure her. To remove the stain of his careless fingerprints with a caress as soft as a feather. To press his mouth to her and kiss away those horrible marks; to make her feel secure and safe under his protection.

But instead he stood silently, woodenly, feeling strangely, achingly hollow as she turned and walked out of the room.

Holly had finished seeing to Sophia and tidying up the kitchen. Not that she'd had to do much, as Julius had loaded the dishwasher and washed up by hand the baking dish she'd cooked the chicken in. It surprised her he knew how to do such mundane stuff. He was from such a wealthy, privileged background. He'd had servants waiting on him all of his life. He wouldn't have had to lift a finger before some servant would have come running and seen to his needs and that of his siblings. And yet he had left the kitchen and the dining room absolutely spotless. The uneaten food was packaged away with cling film in the fridge. The benches had been wiped. The lights were turned down. The blinds were drawn.

Holly was too restless to go to bed. She thought about going for another swim but didn't want to encounter Julius. Well, that was only partly true. She could face him when he was stern and headmaster-ish but, when he got all caring and concerned and...*protective*, it did strange things to her insides. She had never had anyone to protect her. Not since her father had died. No one had ever stood up for her. Everyone was so quick to judge her. They never waited to get to know her, to try and understand the dynamics of her personality and what had formed it. Tragedy, abuse, maltreatment and neglect did not a happy person make. She knew she should try harder to be nicer to people. She knew she should learn to trust people because not everyone was an exploitative creep.

The news of his father's love child was clearly a terrible shock to Julius. Finding out he had a half-sister would have rocked him to the core. He hadn't wanted to discuss it, which she could understand, given his personality. He didn't like surprises. He liked time to think things over. She suspected he would eventually come round to wanting to meet his half-sister. He was too principled simply to pretend she didn't exist.

But the news of the existence of a love child certainly did raise the chance of the press hounding him. He was obviously worried Holly would exploit the situation—dish the dirt on him or make things look salacious between him and her. She might like to rattle his chain for a bit of fun but there was no way she would take her games into the public sphere. She didn't want her stepfather to know where she was. If she drew attention to herself by speaking to the press, who knew what would happen.

Holly wandered along the corridor past the library on her way to her room. The door was slightly ajar and the room was in darkness except for the moonlight shining through the waist-high window. One of the windows must have been mistakenly left open for she could see one of the sheer curtains fluttering on the light breeze coming from outside. She considered leaving it but then remembered Sophia was tucked up in bed upstairs. It would be a shame if it rained overnight and some of those precious books nearest the window were damaged.

Holly moved over to the window without bothering to turn on the light, as the moonlight was like a silver beam across the floor. She closed the window and straightened the breeze-ruffled curtain. She stood there for a long moment looking out at the moonlit gardens and fields beyond. It was such a beautiful property. So peaceful and isolated. There wasn't a neighbour for miles. No wonder Julius loved working and living here. She had spent most of her life in cramped flats in multi-storey buildings with the roar of traffic below and the sound of neighbours packed in on every side. But here it was so serene and peaceful she could hear frogs croaking and owls hooting. It was like listening to a night orchestra. The moonlight cast everything in an opalescent glow that gave the gardens a magical, storybook quality.

It was only when Holly turned around to leave that she saw the silent, seated figure behind the large mahogany leather-topped desk. 'Oh, sorry,' she said, somehow managing to smother her startled gasp. 'I didn't see you there. The light wasn't on so I thought someone must've left the window open. It looks like we could get a storm so I thought I'd better shut it since Sophia's gone to bed.' *Shut up. You're gabbling.*

Julius's leather chair creaked in protest as he rose from behind the desk. 'I'm sorry for giving you a fright.'

'You didn't,' Holly said then, seeing the wry lift of one of his eyebrows added, 'well, maybe a little. Why didn't you say something? Why are you sitting here in the dark?'

'I was thinking.'

'About your family…um…situation?'

'I was thinking about you, actually.'

Her heart gave a stumble. 'Me?' His eyes went to her arms. 'Oh. Well, you said sorry, so it's all good.'

His frowning gaze meshed with hers. 'How can you be so casual about something so serious? I hurt you, Holly. I physically hurt you.'

'You didn't mean to,' Holly said. 'Anyway, it was probably my fault for stirring you up.'

'That's no excuse,' he said. 'It shouldn't matter how much provocation a man receives. No man should ever use physical force. I can never forgive myself for that. I'm disgusted with myself. Truly disgusted.'

Holly rolled her lips together for a moment. 'I've not been the easiest house guest.'

A host of emotions flickered over his face. Emotions she suspected he wasn't used to feeling. It was there in the dark blue of his eyes. It was in the thinned-out line of his sculptured mouth. 'You don't have to be anything but yourself,' he said in a husky tone. 'You're fine just the way you are.'

No one had ever accepted her for who she was. Why would they? She wasn't the sort of person people found acceptable. If it wasn't her background, then it was her behaviour. She rubbed people up the wrong way. How could he say she was fine the way she was? *She* wasn't fine with the way she was.

'So, how are things with your family?' Holly said to fill the heavy silence.

He turned away as he pushed a hand through his hair. 'I haven't been able to contact my sister. The legitimate one, I mean.'

'You're worried about her?'

'A little.'

Holly couldn't help feeling a little envious of Miranda Ravensdale. How wonderful to have a big brother to watch out for you. Two, in fact. Not that she knew if Julius's twin brother, Jake, had the same protective qualities as Julius. She got the impression Jake was a bit of a lad about town.

'Maybe her phone is flat, or she's turned it off or something,' she said.

'Maybe.'

Another silence ticked past.

'Oh, well, then,' Holly said, making a step towards the door. 'I'd better let you get on with it.'

'Holly.'

She turned and looked at him. 'Would you like me to get you a coffee? A night cap or something? Since Sophia's off-duty you'll have to put up with me doing the housekeeper stuff.'

His dark eyes moved over her face, centred on her mouth and then came back to her gaze. 'Only if you'll have one with me.'

Holly chewed the inside of her mouth. She didn't trust herself around him. He was dangerous in this gentle and reflective mood. Keeping her game face on was easy when he was being sarcastic and cynical towards her. But this was different. 'It's a bit late at night for me to drink coffee, and since I don't drink alcohol I'd be pretty boring company...'

His mouth twisted ruefully. 'I suppose I deserve that brush off, don't I?'

'I'm not brushing you off. If I were brushing you off then you'd know about it, let me tell you,' she said.

'I'm not the sort of person to hand out a parachute for anyone's ego.'

He gave a soft laugh, the low, deep sound doing something odd and ticklish to the base of Holly's spine. 'That I can believe.'

There was another beat of silence.

'What would you do if you found out you had a half-sibling?' he asked.

Holly shifted her lips from side to side as she thought about it. 'I would definitely want to meet him or her. I've always wanted a sister or brother. It would've come in handy to have someone to stick up for me.'

He studied her for a long moment. The low light didn't take anything away from his handsome features. If anything, it highlighted them. The aristocratic landscape of his face reminded her of a hero out of a nineteenth-century novel. Dark and brooding; aloof and unknowable.

'Things were pretty tough for you as a kid, weren't they?'

Holly moved her gaze out of reach of his. 'I don't like talking about it.'

'Talking sometimes helps people to understand you a little better.'

'Yeah, well, if people don't like me at "hello" then how is telling them all about my messed-up childhood going to change their opinion?'

'Perhaps if you worked on your first impressions you might win a few friends on your side.'

Holly thought of how she'd stomped into his office that morning—had it really only been a day?—with her verbal artillery blazing. She'd put him on the back foot at the outset. But she'd been angry and churned up over everything. Her forthrightness had been automatic. She liked to get in first before people took advantage. 'I could've come in and been polite as anything but you'd already made up your mind about me. You'd heard about my criminal behaviour. Nothing I could've said or done would've changed your opinion.'

Julius took a step that brought him close to where she was standing. Holly held her breath as he sent a fingertip down the length of her arm, from the top of her shoulder to her wrist. The nerves fluttered like moths beneath her skin. Her heart skipped a beat. Her stomach tilted. 'Are you sure I didn't hurt you?' His voice was low, a deep burr of sound that made the base of her spine fizz.

'I'm sure.'

He sent the same fingertip down the curve of her cheek, outlining her face from just behind her ear to the base of her chin. 'I think underneath that brash exterior is a very frightened little girl.'

Holly quickly disguised a knotty swallow. 'Keep your day job, Julius. You'd make a rubbish therapist.'

His eyes held hers for another long moment. 'I'll see to the rest of the windows,' he said. 'You go on up to bed. Sleep well.'

Like that's going to happen, Holly thought as she turned and slipped out of the room.

Holly didn't see Julius for over a week. He hadn't informed her he was leaving at all. She heard it from Sophia, who told her he was working on some important software and had to attend meetings in Buenos Aires, as well as flying to Santiago in Chile. It annoyed Holly he hadn't bothered to tell her what his schedule was. He could have done so that night in the library, especially as she'd heard him leave the very next morning. But then, she reminded herself, she was just a temporary hindrance for him. The more time away from the villa—*away from her*—the better. The bruises on her arms had faded but the bruise to her ego had not. Why couldn't he have talked to her in person? Told her his plans?

The fact was, it was dead boring without him. Sophia was kind and sweet and did her best to make sure Holly had plenty to do without exploiting her. But spending hours with a middle-aged woman who reminded her too much of the mother she no longer had was not Holly's idea of fun. The more time she spent with the gentle and kind housekeeper, the more she ached for what she had lost. Sophia had a tendency to mother her, to treat her like a surrogate daughter. Holly appreciated the gesture on one level but on another it made her feel unutterably sad.

Which was all the more reason she missed the verbal sparring she'd done with Julius. She missed his tall figure striding down the corridors with a dark frown on his handsome face. She missed the sound of his cultured accent in that mellifluous baritone that did such strange things to her spine. She missed the excitement in her body, the buzzing, thrilling sensation of female desire he triggered every time he looked at her. Her body felt flat and listless without him around to charge it up with energy.

The days dragged with an interminable slowness that made Holly's restlessness close to unbearable. Although she enjoyed the tasks Sophia set her, as the villa was beautiful and full of exquisite works of art and priceless collector's pieces, it just wasn't the same without

Julius there. The nights were even worse. Sophia usually went to bed early, which meant there was no one to talk to. The rest of the villa staff—the gardener and the man who looked after the horses on the property—lived in accommodation separate from the villa. There was only so much television Holly could watch and, even though she enjoyed reading, the evenings were particularly tiresome.

The one thing Julius had done for her since he'd gone away, however, was have some clothes delivered to the villa for her. They were mostly smart-casual separates, as well as a couple of dresses, including a long, slinky formal one made of navy blue silk. There were shoes and underwear the likes of which she had never seen before: cobweb-fine lace, some with fancy little bows and embroidered rosebuds or daisies. There were bathing suits as well, a one-piece black one and a fuchsia-pink bikini.

Make-up and perfume arrived in neat little packages. A hairdresser arrived at the villa and worked on Holly's hair until she barely recognised herself in the mirror. Gone were the pink streaks and split ends. Her wild curls were toned, tamed and cut in a shoulder-length style that could be worn up or down, depending on her mood or the occasion.

But for all the finery Holly felt dissatisfied. What was the point of all these gorgeous clothes if she had no one to see her in them? She didn't even have anywhere to go because she wasn't allowed to leave the premises unless Julius accompanied her as her official guardian. It was part of the diversionary programme's fine print.

Late on Sunday, well after Sophia had retired for the night, Holly turned off the show she had been only half-watching on television and made her way to her room. But on the way past Julius's suite she stopped. She had been in a couple of days ago with Sophia to do a light clean. His suite had a balcony but the doors had been closed and Holly had kept her back to it. She had worked briskly and efficiently with the minimum of talk, desperate to stave off a panic attack if Sophia asked her to dust or sweep out there. If Sophia had sensed anything was amiss, she hadn't said, although Holly suspected there was not much that would escape the housekeeper's attention.

Before Holly could change her mind she turned the handle on the door of the suite and stepped inside. The balcony doors were closed and locked, the gauzy curtains pulled across the windows. Even though the room had been empty for days, Holly could still smell the lemon and lime notes of Julius's aftershave. She turned on one of the bedside lamps rather than the top light in case Sophia saw the spill of light from her room on the top floor.

The forbidden nature of what Holly was doing made a frisson of excitement shiver over her flesh. This was where Julius slept. This was where Julius made love with his occasional lovers. The lovers Sophia stalwartly, stubbornly, refused to comment on or reveal any information about. Holly had looked on the internet on the library's computer for any press items on him but there was virtually nothing about his private life. There was stuff about Julius's work in astrophysics and about his software company that had come about after he had designed a special computer programme used on the space telescopes in the Atacama Desert and which had turned him into a multi-millionaire overnight.

There was plenty of stuff about his father's love-child scandal. Every newsfeed was running with it. There was also plenty of information on Julius's twin, Jake. Jake was the epitome of the 'love them and leave them' playboy: the 'Prince of Pickups' as one article described him. It was uncanny seeing the likeness to Julius. They were mirror images of each other. She wondered if she met them together if she would be able to tell them apart. The only slight difference she could see was in every photo Jake was smiling as if that was his default position. Julius, on the other hand, was not one to smile so readily. He was serious in demeanour and nature. He was conservative where, from what some of the photos suggested, his twin was a boundary-pusher—a born risk-taker.

Holly wandered about Julius's suite, stopping to check out a photo of his younger sister on his dressing table. Miranda was pretty in a pixyish, girl-next-door sort of way. She was petite with porcelain-white skin and auburn hair. Nothing like her extraordinarily beautiful mother, Elisabetta Albertini, Holly duly noted. She put the photo down and stepped over to the walk-in wardrobe, hesitating for a nanosecond before she slid the door back and walked inside.

All of his shirts, suits and jackets were in neat rows. His sweaters were folded in symmetrical colour-coordinated stacks. His shoes were all polished and paired and perfectly aligned on the tiered shoe rack.

She picked a pair of cufflinks up from the waist-high shelf above a bank of drawers. The cufflinks were a designer brand with diamonds in the shape of a J. She wondered if he had bought them for himself or whether they had been a gift from a member of his family. Mi-

randa, perhaps? The photo of her in his room suggested
he adored her. It was the only photo she had seen of any
of his family in the villa.

The sound of a footfall in the bedroom startled Holly
so much she felt her flesh shrink away from her skeleton. She slipped into the shadows of Julius's suits, using
them as a shield to hide behind. Her heart hammered.
Her breath halted. She couldn't allow Julius to find her
in here. But how on earth was she going to get out? Why
hadn't he told her and Sophia he was coming home tonight? Why turn up unannounced? What if he went to
bed while she was stuck here, hiding in his wardrobe?
She would have to hope and pray he'd go to the en suite
and have a shower or something so she could sneak out
without being detected. Hopefully the fact his bedside
lamp was on wouldn't make him suspicious. He might
think Sophia had left it on in anticipation of him coming home...or something.

The thoughts were a tumbling mess inside her head.
Round and round they went until she felt dizzy. Her
skin was breaking out in a sweat. She could feel beads
of it rolling down between her breasts, under her arms,
across her top lip.

'Holly?' Sophia's voice called out. 'Is that you?'

The relief Holly felt was so great it was as if her legs
were going to fold beneath her as the tension washed out
of her. Even her arms felt boneless, her shoulders dropping as if had just been relieved of carrying a tremen-
dous weight. She took a steadying breath and walked
out of the wardrobe with what she hoped was a calm,
collected and innocent look on her face. 'Sorry,' she
said. 'Did I give you a scare?'

Sophia was frowning. 'What were you doing in Señor Ravensdale's wardrobe?'

'I was just…checking to see if I'd put his shirts I ironed the other day in the right place,' Holly said, mentally marvelling at her ability to construct a credible excuse at such short notice. 'You know how fussy he is. I didn't want him to come home and get antsy about the blue shirts mixed up with the white ones. Oh, and I straightened his ties. One was hanging half a millimetre lower than the others.'

Sophia's frown lessened slightly but didn't completely disappear. 'You don't have to work at this time of night. You're entitled to time off.'

'I know, but I was bored, so I thought I'd double-check stuff.'

'You've worked hard this week,' Sophia said. 'Much harder than I thought you would.'

'Yeah, well, I'm not afraid of hard work,' Holly said. 'So, why are you up? I thought you were in bed.'

'My wrist is giving me a bit of pain,' Sophia said, wincing as she cradled her arm against her body. 'I was coming past to go downstairs to make a hot drink when I heard a sound.'

'Weren't you worried it might be a burglar?'

'No, I knew it was you.'

'How?'

'I could smell your perfume,' Sophia said. 'The one Señor Ravensdale bought for you. It was a good choice. It suits you.'

Holly gave the housekeeper a quick stretch of her lips as a smile. 'That man has serious class. Does he always buy women such expensive gifts?'

Sophia gave her the sort of reproachful look a parent would give to a persistently naughty child. 'Come and make me a hot chocolate,' she said. 'Then it's time, young lady, for bed.'

'When is Julius coming home?' Holly asked as they walked down to the kitchen together. 'Have you heard from him?'

'He sent a text a couple of hours ago,' Sophia said. 'His plane was delayed in Santiago.'

'Maybe he's catching up with a lady friend.'

Sophia pursed her lips without responding.

'Why do you call him "Señor" instead of Julius?' Holly asked.

'He's my employer.'

'I know but you and he seem to be pretty chummy,' Holly said. 'How long have you worked for him?'

'Since he moved to Argentina eight years ago.'

'So you would've seen quite a few girlfriends come and go in his life, huh?'

Sophia cast her a glance. 'Why are you so interested in his private life? Do you have designs on him?'

Holly coughed out a laugh. 'Me? Interested in him? Are you joking? He's the last person I would fall for. The very last.'

Sophia released a soft sigh. 'That's probably a good thing.'

'Because I'm too far below his station?'

Sophia shook her head. 'No. He wouldn't let something like that be an issue. I think he wouldn't fall in love too easily, that's all.'

'Like we have a choice in these things,' Holly said, then quickly added, 'not that I'm speaking from experience or anything.'

'So you haven't lost your heart to anyone yet?' Sophia asked with another sideways glance.

The word *yet* seemed to hang in the air. It was like a gauntlet being thrown down. Fate issuing a challenge. A dare.

Holly laughed again. 'Not yet.' *Not ever. Not going to happen.*

Not in a million years.

CHAPTER EIGHT

JULIUS HADN'T PLANNED to drive home so late but his flight back to Buenos Aires from Santiago had been delayed several hours due to a storm. A solid week of work, long hours of meetings and field research had done little to quell the errant feelings he had for Holly. Feelings he hadn't expected to feel. Didn't want to feel. She occupied his thoughts whenever his mind drifted away from work. She filled his brain. She filled his body with forbidden desires and wicked urges. She filled his every waking moment—and even his dreams—with visions of her lithe body, her pert breasts, her cheeky smile and the way she upped her chin in a challenge or twinkled her brown eyes in a dare.

He could not remember a time when he had been more obsessed with a woman. She was as far from an ideal partner as any he could imagine. Her wilfulness, her defiance and her rebellious nature made everything that was rational, logical and intellectual inside him shrink away in abject horror. But everything that was male and primal in him wanted to possess her. He ached and pulsed to feel her body, to be surrounded by her. Every hormone in his body twanged with longing. Every nerve-ending craved the stroke or glide of her touch. He had X-rated dreams about her pouty little mouth on him, drawing on him, pleasuring...

Julius was disgusted with himself. Not just because of his uncontrollable desire for her but because he still couldn't forgive himself for the way he had hurt her. What had he been thinking, hauling her bodily from the pool like that? There was *no* excuse. So what if she had goaded him? So what if she had defied him? Disobeyed him? He was an adult. He was a civilised, educated man. What had he hoped his action would achieve?

Or had he secretly—*unconsciously*—wanted to touch her? To hold her sexy, wet body against the throbbing heat of his...

He had wanted to kiss her so badly it had tortured him not to. Her mouth had been so close he'd felt the breeze of her sweet breath. It had taken every ounce of self-control he possessed and then some to drop his hold on her and step back. He could still feel the silk of her skin against his fingers. He could still feel the magnetic force of her body drawing his closer. It was stronger, way more powerful than anything he had ever felt before. How he had not slammed his mouth down on hers and thrust his tongue through her lush lips still surprised him.

He had been so close.

So terrifyingly, shamefully close.

Work had legitimately called him away, thankfully. He hadn't trusted himself to be around her. He still didn't trust himself, which was even more worrying.

But it wasn't just the physical attraction that was so troubling to him. There were other feelings he was experiencing that were far more dangerous. Tiny sprouts of affection were popping up inside him. He actually *liked* her. He admired her spirit. Her edginess. Her blatant disregard for the rules. For propriety. He found himself missing her teasing playfulness. He missed her dimpled smile and the way her eyes danced with mischief.

He had no business missing her. He wasn't supposed to get attached to her. She wasn't his type. And he clearly wasn't hers. She only wanted to sleep with him to prove a point. It was nothing but a game to her.

He was nothing but a game to her.

Another bonus of being called away to work was that the press had stayed away from his villa. He had been intercepted at the airport and issued his usual 'no comment' response to the media. The last thing he wanted was the press sniffing around his home and finding a young woman in residence, especially as he didn't trust Holly to behave herself. He'd left strict instructions with Sophia on monitoring Holly's movements and making sure she didn't speak to anyone if they should turn up at the villa. No one had, which gave him some measure of comfort, but how long before someone did?

Julius parked in the garage and walked into the villa as quietly as he could so as not to disturb anyone. It was two in the morning so he hoped his little house guest was tucked away safely in bed.

She wasn't.

Holly came out of the kitchen as he came in the back door. She was wearing one of the outfits he'd bought her. The cashmere separates looked far slinkier on her than it had in the online catalogue. But then she would make a bin liner look like a designer gown, he thought. The fabric draped her slim curves like the skin of an evening glove.

'How was your trip?' she asked.

Julius wasn't in the mood for trite conversation. Not with her looking good enough to eat and swallow whole. How did she manage to stir him up so easily? 'Tiring.'

She moved towards him with catlike grace. 'Fancy a snack?'

'What's on the menu?' *Bad choice of words.*

Her eyes glinted. 'What do you fancy?'

He tried not to look at her mouth but a force far more powerful than his resolve pulled his gaze to its lush ripeness. 'What's on offer?' What was it with him and the double entendres? He was acting like Jake, for God's sake.

'Whatever you want,' she said. 'Your wish is my command.'

'I thought you didn't take too kindly to commands?'

She tiptoed her fingers along the corded muscles of his arm. 'Maybe I'll make an exception tonight.'

He suppressed a shiver as her fingers lit every nerve under his skin with red-hot fire. Need pulsed in his groin. Lust growled, roared. 'Why?'

'Because I've missed you.'

Julius barked out a laugh and gently pushed her arm away as he moved past. 'Go to bed.'

'Why didn't you tell me you were going away?'

He turned back to look at her. 'You're answerable to me. Not me to you. Or has that somehow slipped your attention?'

Her caramel-brown eyes ran over him like a lick of flame. 'Were you with a lover?'

He gritted his teeth until his jaw ground together like two tectonic plates. 'No. I was working. Remember that word you seem to have so much difficulty with?'

She leaned one shoulder against the door jamb. 'I've been working. Go ask Sophia.'

'I will, but not at this time in the morning.'

Her eyes did another scan of his body, her chin coming to rest at a haughty height. 'I even cleaned your room.'

Julius didn't like the thought of her in his room. Actually, he liked the thought way too much. His mind filled with images of her laid out on his bed, her gorgeous, luscious body as hungry for him as he was for her. His flesh crawled with lust. It was like a fever in his blood. Raging. Taking him. Taking over his control like a shot of a powerful drug. 'I'd prefer it if you'd stay out of there.'

'Why?' she said. 'You let Sophia change your bed. Why shouldn't I?'

Because I want you in it, not changing it, he thought with a savage wave of self-disgust. 'I trust you left everything as you found it?' he said.

Her brows drew together. 'What's that supposed to mean?'

'I seem to recall your rap sheet includes theft.'

'So?'

'So I want you to keep your hands clean.'

Her top lip curved up on one side. 'Don't worry,' she said. 'You have nothing I want.'

'Only my body.'

A dark, triumphant glint shone in her gaze. 'Not as much as you want mine.'

'You think?'

'I know.'

Julius wanted to prove he could resist her. He *needed* to prove it, if not to her then to himself. He reached for her, encircling her wrists with his fingers. Holding her. Securing her. Her eyes widened but not in fear. He could read her signals as easily as she read his. Mutual desire ran between them like the shock of an electric current. He could feel it through her flesh where it was in contact with his. He looked at her mouth and watched as she ran the tip of her tongue over her lips, leaving a glistening sheen.

Her eyelashes came down over her eyes, her breath dancing over his lips as she rose on tiptoe. He felt the brush of her body against his just before her mouth touched his. He didn't move. Didn't respond. Willed himself not to respond. Her tongue licked his top lip and then his lower one. The tantalising friction set his nerves screaming for more but still he stayed statue-still.

She came at him again, her tongue sweeping over his lower lip in a drugging caress that made his groin tighten to the point of pain. The need to taste her, to take control of the kiss, was like an unstoppable tide. He let out a muttered swear word as he splayed his hands through her hair and covered her mouth with his.

Her lips were soft and full, her mouth tasting of chocolate, milk and temptation. He drove his tongue through her parted lips, plundering her mouth, seeking her tongue to tangle with it in a duel that made the blood pump all the harder in his veins. She made a sexy little sound of approval as he pulled her closer to his body, letting her feel his hardness, the need he couldn't hide even if he'd wanted to.

Julius succoured on her mouth as if it was his only source of sustenance. She was a drug he hadn't known he had a taste for until now. He was lethally addicted to her. His body craved hers. Ached for hers. He pulled at her lower lip with his teeth, taking little nips and bites before using his tongue to salve where he had been. She responded with her own little series of playful bites, not just on his mouth, but also on his neck, and his earlobes, sucking on them until he thought he was going to disgrace himself. He shivered as her tongue came back to play with his, in and outside of their mouths in little flicks and thrusts of lust.

He took charge again by backing her up against the wall, his hands shaping her curves as his mouth crushed hers. She made a little whimpering sound as one of his hands cupped her breast. She moved against him, a gesture of encouragement he was in no state to resist. He shoved aside her top and bra to access her naked flesh. He brought his mouth down to suckle on her erect nipple before he swirled his tongue around her areole. He kissed his way over her breast, lingering on the underside when he heard her gasp as if he had found a particularly sensitive erogenous zone.

The skin there was as soft and smooth as silk. He trailed his tongue like a rasp along that scented curve, his senses in overload as he thought of how much he wanted to possess her. It was a driving force in his body. A primal urge he had no hope of controlling. His desire was a wild, primitive beast that had broken free of its chains and was now on the rampage.

Julius uncovered her other breast and subjected it to the same sensual assault, breathing in the fragrance of her body—a mixture of the flowery perfume he had bought her and her own bewitching female scent. The scent that was filling his nostrils, making him crazy, making him want her more than he had wanted anyone.

He left her breasts to come back to her mouth, driving his tongue through the seam of her lips, as he wanted to drive through the seam of her body. She gave a breathless whimper and reached between their hard-pressed bodies to uncover him. Her hands were on his belt buckle and then his zip, but he didn't do anything to stop her. It was too intoxicating to feel those wicked little hands moving over him, releasing him, stroking him, pleasuring him.

He smothered a rough curse as her thumb caressed the sensitive head of his erection while her mouth played with his. He had never had a more exciting encounter. He wanted to feel her mouth on him, to have her submit to his wildest fantasies.

And, as if she was acting a role scripted right from his imagination, she sank to her knees in front of him, cupping him, breathing over him with her dancing breath, her moist tongue poised.

He put a hand on the top of her head and pulled back. 'No,' he said. 'You don't have to do that.'

She looked up at him questioningly. 'But I thought all guys...?'

'It's not safe without a condom,' Julius said.

She got to her feet, pushing a strand of her hair back behind one of her ears as she did so. 'That's a first.'

He frowned as he thought of all the men who had been with her. How many? Did it matter? Who was he to judge? He'd had his share of sexual encounters. Not as many as his brother, but enough to forget times, places and, yes, even some names.

But there would be no forgetting Holly Perez, he thought. The taste of her was still fizzing on his tongue.

The feel of her was still tingling in his fingertips. His need of her was still firing in his blood.

'Holly.'

She rounded on him with a combative look. 'So who won that round, do you think? I kissed you but you took it to another level.'

Julius blew out a jagged breath. 'That should never have happened.'

Her chin inched up, her eyes flashing at him. 'You want me but you hate yourself for it, don't you?'

'I don't want to complicate my life, or indeed yours.'

'That wasn't the message I was getting a few minutes ago when you had your mouth on my breast—'

'Will you stop it, for God's sake?' Julius said. 'This is not going to happen, okay?'

Her brown eyes shone with a victorious gleam. 'It already did,' she said, moving up so close he could feel her breasts against his chest. 'You're not going to get that wild animal back in its cage any time soon, are you, Julius?'

He looked down at the tempting curve of her sinful mouth. The mouth he had savaged, pillaged and supped on like a starving man. The luscious and deliciously ripe mouth that had offered to pleasure him. *God strike him down for wanting her to.* He put his hands on her hips to gently push her back from him but then his right hand felt a cube-shaped ridge against her hip. 'What's that in your pocket?'

Her expression faltered for a moment before she tried to move away. 'What? Oh...nothing.'

Julius held her steady, his hands anchoring her so she had to face him. 'Empty your pockets.'

Her eyes flickered with something that looked suspiciously like panic. 'Why?'

'Because I asked you to.'

'Just because you asked me doesn't mean I'll—'

Julius held her left hip with one hand while he dug in her right pocket with the other. He pulled out the cufflinks Miranda had bought him for his last birthday, holding them right in front of Holly's defiant face. 'Want to tell me how they got in there?'

Her teeth sank into her bottom lip. Her eyes skittered away from his. 'I—I can explain...'

He dropped his hands from her as if she was burning him. Which she was. Burning him. Exploiting him. *Stealing* from him while his back was turned. How could he have thought she might not be as bad as she acted? How could he have been so stupid as to feel *affection* for her? What an idiot he was. How could he have let her fool him into believing she was worthy of a second chance? She wasn't just deceitful—she was dangerous. He was nuts to have let her get under his guard. She was a liar and a thief and he'd been too damn close to getting caught in her sugar-coated web.

'I want you out of here by morning,' he said. 'I don't want to hear your explanation. There isn't an explanation you could give that would satisfy me.'

'I was in your walk-in wardrobe earlier tonight.'

'Doing what?'

'Straightening your ties.'

Julius laughed. 'What? You can't do better than that?'

Her chin came up to a pugnacious height. 'I got caught off-guard when Sophia came in unexpectedly. I panicked. I hid in your wardrobe as I thought it was you. I didn't realise I'd put the cufflinks into my pocket until just now. I honestly don't remember doing it. It must've been an impulse or…or something…'

He rolled his eyes. 'Do you really think I'm *that* stupid?'

She bit her lower lip again. 'I know it looks bad…'

'Why were you in my room?'

She shrugged one of her shoulders. 'I was having a look around.'

'For what?' he said. 'Loose change?'

She gave him a gimlet glare. 'I know you think I'm nothing but a petty thief but I didn't take them on purpose. It was an…an accident.'

Julius gave another cynical laugh. 'Yes, Officer,' he said in a parody of her voice. 'I was just walking past Mr Ravensdale's wardrobe and the diamond cufflinks fell into my pocket *by accident.*'

Holly set her mouth. 'I don't care what you think. I know I didn't steal them and that's all that matters.'

'Actually,' Julius said. 'It's not all that matters. Your caseworker will ask me when she calls in the morning and I'll have to tell her you've been stealing.'

Her eyes blazed as they met his. 'Tell her. See if I care.'

She did care. Julius was sure of it. He came to stand in front of her, close enough to feel the heat of her body emanating towards his. He picked up a handful of her hair close to her scalp, making her feel each strand pulling as he brought her mouth close to his. He let his breath mingle with hers, teasing her with the promise of what was to come. 'Here's where your little game backfires, *querida*,' he said. 'You want me just as much as I want you. You weren't expecting that, were you? You thought this would be a one-sided game but it's not.'

Her body brushed against his, by intention or chance he couldn't quite tell. But he saw the reaction on her face—the flicker of want that flashed across her features. The way her pupils dilated, the way her tongue sneaked out to moisten her lips. 'Get your hands off me,' she said.

'When I'm good and ready.' He brought his mouth even closer, breathing in the scent of her, bumping noses with her, nudging her with his chin, rasping his tongue along the seam of her mouth. Teasing her the way she had teased him. He heard her sharp intake of breath as his tongue stroked harder, more insistently. He could feel the struggle in her. The will she had to resist him was faltering just as his had faltered in him. She leaned towards him, her mouth open, her hands on his chest, not flat in the effort of pushing him away, but her fingers curling into the front of his shirt as if she never wanted to let him go.

He allowed himself one touchdown on her mouth. But one wasn't enough. How could he have thought it would ever be enough? Her mouth flowered open even further beneath the light pressure of his until he was suddenly swept up in a passionate exchange that had his blood thundering all over again.

Her tongue entwined with his, her arms looped around his neck, drawing him closer. His hands went to her neat behind, holding her against his throbbing heat. Her breasts were pushed against his chest so hard he could feel her pert nipples through the layers of their clothes.

Her hand reached between their bodies and stroked the hardened length of him, inciting his lust to fever pitch. He did the same to her, outlining her feminine form with the stroke of his fingers until she was breathing as hard as him. He took it one step further, driven by an urge he couldn't control. He tugged her trousers down past her hips so he could access her naked skin. He slipped one finger inside her, his control almost blowing when he felt how hot and wet and tight she was. She gasped and moved against his hand in a plea that needed no language other than the one their bodies were speaking. He stroked the bud of her core with the pad of his thumb, feeling it swell and peak under the pressure of his touch.

She suddenly gripped his shoulders and arched up as she convulsed. Violently. Repeatedly. He felt every contraction of her orgasm. Watched as the pleasure rose in a tidal glow over her face.

He kissed her mouth. Hard. Passionately. Swallowing the last of her breathless gasps as the aftermath of release flowed through her.

But then she slipped out of his hold, not quite able to hold his gaze. Her hands pulled up her trousers and fixed her gaping shirt before going across her body in a defensive, keep-away-from-me pose.

'Holly...'

She gave him a tight smile that didn't reach her eyes. 'What's the protocol here? Should I say thanks? Or offer to do you in return?'

He let out a long breath. 'That won't be necessary.'

'Well, thanks anyway,' she said. 'I didn't know I had it in me to get off like that. That's quite some technique you've got there.'

Julius scraped a hand through his hair. 'I shouldn't have taken things that far.'

'No problemo,' she said. 'I enjoyed it, as you could probably tell. Which is another first.'

He frowned. 'What do you mean?'

'I've never had an orgasm with a guy before.'

'Never?'

'No, but don't tell any of my ex-partners that,' she said. 'You know how fragile the male ego is.'

'How many partners have you had?'

'Four. Five, if you count yourself,' she said. 'But does that count, since you didn't actually put your...?'

'No,' Julius said. 'It doesn't.'

She shifted her lips from side to side. 'So, are we done here?'

He moved far enough away from her so he wouldn't be tempted to touch her. 'I'll see you in the morning. Goodnight.'

'You mean you're not sending me on my way to prison after all?'

Julius clenched his jaw. 'I'm giving you one more chance.' He hoped he wouldn't regret it.

She walked to the door to leave but at the last moment turned and looked at him. 'If I'd wanted to pinch your cufflinks, do you think I'd be carrying them around in my pocket?'

'Maybe you haven't had time to hide them in your room.'

Her eyes held his without shame. Without flinching. 'I had time to do lots of things. I could've called the press, for instance. I could've given them an exclusive.'

'Why didn't you?'

She gave one of her cute little lip-shrugs. 'I don't like it when people say stuff about me that isn't true, so why would I do that to someone else?'

Julius had measured the risks when he'd left to go away for work. But he'd figured Sophia would keep things in check. His housekeeper guarded his privacy almost more zealously than he did himself. But it was true Holly could have made things difficult for him. She could have made herself a small fortune. All it would have taken was a phone call. Why hadn't she? It wouldn't even have broken her probation conditions. Had he misjudged her? Or was this a clever ploy of hers, to get him to trust her before she went for broke? 'Thank you for acting so…honourably,' he said.

Her features took on a cynical cast. 'Haven't you heard there's honour amongst thieves?'

'But you keep insisting you're not a thief.'

'I'm not.'

Julius wanted to believe her. He wasn't sure why. Maybe to reassure himself he wasn't harbouring a criminal under his roof. Maybe so he could justify his growing affection for her. Something about the way she held herself, the stubborn pride he could see glittering in her gaze as it held his, made him wonder if he wasn't the only one to have misjudged her. He knew enough about the legal system to know the courts did not always serve justice. Attack-dog lawyers could swing a case. Evidence could be planted. Reputations ruined by innuendo. Holly had no money, no way of defending herself against a powerful lawyer. She had already hinted about the bleakness of her background. What chance would someone like her have against a system that favoured those with unlimited money and power at their disposal?

'It's late,' he said. 'You should've been in bed hours ago.'

'By the way, thanks for the clothes and make-up and stuff.'

'You're welcome,' he said. 'Your hair looks nice, by the way.'

'Much more acceptable, huh?'

'It was fine the way it was, but I thought—'

'It's fine, Julius,' she said with another stiff smile. 'Do you airbrush all of your girlfriends?'

'You are not my girlfriend. And, no, I do not.'

There was an odd little silence.

Julius watched as she sank her teeth into her lower lip as if she had suddenly found herself out of her depth. Had he offended her by organising a hairdresser? Sophia had suggested it, but now that he thought about it, maybe it had sent the wrong message. Had the clothes also been too much? Had he made her feel she wasn't acceptable without fine feathers? He thought he'd been helping her. She'd been bathing in her underwear. Surely it was the decent thing to do, to buy her appropriate clothing? The make-up and perfume… Well, didn't all girls enjoy that sort of stuff? She had come with so little luggage. Just a beaten-up backpack that hardly looked big enough to carry anything. Surely it hadn't been wrong to give her a few things to make her feel better about herself…or was he trying to make himself feel better about those fingerprints on her arms?

His gut clenched sickeningly as he thought of how easily she could have exploited him. All it would have taken was a photo of those bruises and a call to a nosy journalist and his reputation would have been shot. She'd had the perfect opportunity to get back at him, yet she hadn't. The week had passed without incident. Sophia had informed him Holly had been a perfect house guest, going out of her way to be helpful.

A good girl…

Not a moment's trouble...

'If you say you didn't intend to steal the cufflinks, then I believe you.' It was only once Julius said the words that he believed they were true. Her explanation was perfectly reasonable. She could have been startled and slipped them into her pocket without realising. How many times had he done the same with his keys when something or someone distracted him?

Or was he looking for a way to keep her with him?

It was a shock to think his motives were perhaps not as altruistic as they ought to be. The energy he felt with Holly, the electric buzz of sensation and thrill of her, overrode everything that was logical and responsible in him.

Her eyes widened momentarily before narrowing. 'Why?'

'I just do.'

She dropped her gaze from his. 'Thank you.' Her voice was just a thread of sound. Then she seemed to gather herself and brought her eyes back to his for a brief moment. 'Well, goodnight, then,' she said and left him with just the lingering scent of her fragrance to haunt his senses.

CHAPTER NINE

HOLLY CLOSED THE door to her bedroom and leaned back against it as she let out a long, shuddering breath. Julius *believed* her. He actually believed she hadn't tried to steal those wretched cufflinks. She hadn't registered she'd put them there, or at least not consciously. It had been a knee-jerk reaction to being discovered in his room. She must have slipped them into her pocket when she'd first heard Sophia and forgotten about them.

But Julius said he believed her.

How could he? She would never have believed him if the tables had been turned. But then, she was cynical. She didn't trust anyone. She was always on guard, always watching out for someone to take advantage, to rip her off or exploit her.

Was Julius different? Was he the sort of person to suspend judgement until reliable evidence came in?

Holly wondered if she had done herself a disservice by antagonising him so much. He might turn out to be the best ally she had ever had. But from the moment she had met him she had put him off-side. Winding him up, needling him, making him believe things about her that weren't true.

Was it too late to turn things around? Could she even

bother? She would only be here another couple of weeks and then she'd be gone. It had never worked for her to get too attached to anyone or any place. They always changed. People changed. Circumstances changed. One minute she would feel marginally secure and then the rug would be ripped out from beneath her and she would hit the hard, cold floor. This time with Julius in his flash villa was a temporary thing. There would be no point in getting too comfortable. He hadn't even wanted her here in the first place. She was a burden he had to bear.

Why was she always a burden?

Why couldn't someone want her in spite of all her faults? In spite of all her failings? In spite of all her stupid impulses that caused her more trouble than she wanted?

Her body was still firing with the sensations Julius had made her feel. Cataclysmic sensations she had never felt before. He had barely touched her and she had gone off like a firecracker. But he had remained in control. She had even offered to pleasure him and he'd held back. She still couldn't understand why she had done that. Why she had felt such an urgent desire to take him in her mouth bewildered her. She loathed oral sex. The musky, stale scent of a man usually nauseated her.

But with him it was different.

He wasn't musky and stale. He was fresh and intoxicating in his maleness. She had wanted to explore him, to pleasure him, to make him buckle at the knees in the same way he had done to her. But he hadn't insisted on her doing it. He hadn't pressured her.

He'd *protected* her by his restraint.

He'd pleasured her without wanting or insisting on anything in return. Even now she could feel the aftershock tremors moving through her body, awakening more news: new needs, needs that wanted—craved and hungered—to be assuaged. Maybe that was his power trip. Maybe that was his way of keeping a step in front of her. Maybe his self-control was superior after all. Far more superior than she'd thought.

Something had changed in their relationship…something she couldn't quite put her finger on. No one had given her the benefit of the doubt before. No one.

No one had made her feel the things Julius made her feel. No one.

No one had seen behind the mask she wore to the person she wanted to be.

No one.

When Holly came downstairs to organise breakfast the following morning, Sophia was already up and about. 'I'm going to spend a few days with my sister,' Sophia said. 'You're doing so well managing things here I thought I'd make the most of it by having some time off. Maria's picking me up in a few minutes.'

Holly frowned. 'Is Julius okay with that? I mean, leaving me in charge?'

'He's the one who suggested it.'

Holly's frown deepened. 'Really?'

Sophia nodded. 'He's also worried I might be tempted to do too much. I think he's right. I have been overdoing it. But this little break will help.'

'But what will Natalia have to say?' Holly said. 'Aren't you supposed to be the one mentoring me?'

Sophia's expression turned to one of concern. 'Would you rather I didn't go? I can cancel if you like. I'm sure my sister won't mind.'

'No, don't do that. I'm just wondering about the pro-gramme.' *And being left alone in the villa with Julius without a chaperone.*

'Señor Ravensdale is the one who is ultimately re-sponsible for you,' Sophia said. 'I'm here as a guide but you don't need me. In many ways you're more compe-tent than me. Your cooking is restaurant standard. I'm the one who should be taking lessons off you.'

'Yeah, well, it's easy to cook nice things when you have access to top quality ingredients,' Holly said.

Sophia smiled. 'Would you mind taking Señor Ra-vensdale's breakfast to him? He's in the morning room upstairs.'

'Sure.'

'Ah, that's Maria's car now.' Sofia gave her one last smile and left.

Holly waited for the coffee to percolate before she put it on the tray to take upstairs. The morning room was on the second level of the villa, which wasn't con-venient to the kitchen in terms of serving breakfast, but it had a lovely easterly aspect overlooking the gar-dens and the lake. She had been in a couple of times to dust and vacuum. It was decorated in soft yellows and cream with a touch of blue, giving it a fresh energetic look perfect for the start of the day.

When Holly shouldered open the door, a quake of dread moved through her. The French doors leading to the balcony were wide open. Julius was sitting in a patch of sunlight at the wrought-iron table with some papers set in front of him. The slight breeze was ruf-fling the pages, and she watched as one of his hands reached out to anchor them.

He must have sensed her presence, or maybe he heard

the slight rattle of the cup in the saucer on the tray she was carrying, for he looked up. 'Good morning.'

Holly swallowed a bird's nest of panic. Fear crawled over her scalp. Her blood chilled, freezing in her veins until she was certain her heart would stop. Her feet were nailed to the floor. She couldn't move. She was frozen.

Julius frowned. 'What's wrong?'

'Nothing.' Holly took a step forward but couldn't go any farther. 'Um, would you come and get this? I've left something on the hob downstairs.'

'Why don't you come back and join me?' he said as he took the tray from her and placed it on the table on the balcony.

'No thanks.'

'Got out of the wrong side of the bed, did we?'

'Wasn't in it long enough,' she said with a little scowl.

He surveyed her features for a beat or two. 'Come on and join me once you've turned off the hob. It's a lovely morning. There's enough food and coffee here for both of us. Just get another cup and saucer.'

'I said no.'

Julius shrugged as if he didn't care either way. 'Suit yourself.'

'Could you bring the tray back down when you're done?' Holly said as she got to the door.

He turned around to look at her. 'Isn't that your job?'

She held his penetrating look. 'Is that why you've sent Sophia away? What is it about having someone wait on you that gives you such a thrill? Is it the power? The authority? The ego trip?'

A frown tugged at his brow. 'Doesn't the fact I asked

you to join me for breakfast demonstrate I'm not on any power trip?'

She crossed her arms and sent him a hard glare. 'So what was last night all about, then?'

He let out a rough-sounding breath. 'Last night was… I was wrong to let things get to that point,' he said. 'I'm sorry.'

Holly wasn't ready to be mollified. She was still feeling annoyed he'd been able to prove his point so easily. He had won that round. She had responded to him like a sex-starved fool. Which was basically what she was, but still…

He came to where she was standing. He didn't touch her but was close enough for her to feel the tempting warmth of his body. His dark-blue eyes held hers in a gentle lock that made her wonder if he was seeing much more than she wanted him to see. She tried to keep her expression blank but she wasn't quite able to stop her tongue from quickly moistening her lips. She watched as his gaze dipped to follow the movement before coming back to reconnect with hers.

'This thing we have…' he began.

'What thing?'

'I've never met someone who's got my attention quite the way you have,' he said.

'Well, they wouldn't have a chance with you locked away in your mansion with no social life to speak of, now, would they?'

He gave her a wry hint of a smile. 'I get out when I need to.'

'When was the last time you—' Holly put her fingers up in air-quotation-marks '—got out?'

'I had a brief relationship a few months back.'

'Who was she? What was she like?'

'Someone I met at a conference in Santiago,' he said. 'She was beautiful, well educated, came from a good family. She had a nice personality...'

'I'm hearing a big "but".'

'No chemistry.'

'Not good.'

'Definitely not good.' He brushed a stray strand of hair back from her forehead. It was the lightest touch but it made every nerve in her body shudder in delight. Had anyone ever touched her as gently? Had anyone ever looked at her so intently? As if they wanted to see right into the very heart of her?

'So who broke it off?' Holly said. 'You or her?'

'Me.'

'Was she disappointed?'

'If she was, it can't have lasted long as she got engaged a few weeks later to a guy she'd been dating before me.'

'You win some, you lose some.'

His eyes did that back-and-forth searching thing with each of hers. 'It would be highly inappropriate for me to get involved with you,' he said. 'You do understand that, don't you?'

'We're both consenting adults.'

His finger traced the underside of her jaw in a feather-light touch. 'It's not a matter of consent. It's a matter of convention.'

Holly twisted her mouth in a cynical manner. 'Oh, right—the upstairs, downstairs thing.'

He frowned. 'That's not what I meant at all. It wouldn't reflect well on me if I were to engage in a relationship with you. It would look like I'm exploiting you.'

'But making me fetch and carry and ordering me about doesn't?'

He dropped his hand from her face. 'You really suit your name. I don't think I've ever met anyone more prickly.'

'Your breakfast is getting cold,' Holly said, nodding towards his abandoned tray out on the balcony.

Julius narrowed his gaze in thoughtful contemplation. His forehead was lined like tidemarks on the seashore. She could almost hear the cogs of his brain going around. 'You don't have anything on the hob, do you?'

Holly tried to disguise a swallow. His dark blue gaze was probing. Like a strong light shining into the outer limits of her soul. 'No...'

'So unless it's my company there's some other reason you don't want to have breakfast with me on the balcony,' he said in a tone that sounded as if he was thinking out loud.

A loaded silence passed.

Holly let out a shaky sigh. 'I have a...a thing about balconies.'

'You're scared of heights?' He didn't say it in a mocking way. He simply stated it as if it was perfectly reasonable for her to be scared and he wouldn't judge her for it.

Holly felt something hard and tight slip away from her heart. As if a rigid band had come undone. 'Not heights, specifically. Just balconies.'

He took one of her hands and held it in the shelter of his. His thumb stroked the back of her hand in a slow, soothing motion. 'That's why you didn't want the room Sophia prepared for you, isn't it?'

Holly pressed her lips together. Hard. She never spoke to anyone about this stuff. It was stuff she had locked away. But for some reason Julius's gentle tone picked the lock of her determination. He had unravelled the tightly bound knot of her stubborn pride. She released another sigh. 'I got locked out on the balcony when I was a kid,' she said. 'It was something my stepfather thought was entertaining. Seeing me out there in all sorts of weather. He wouldn't let me come in until I said sorry for whatever I'd supposedly done. Not that I ever did much; I only had to look at him a certain way and he'd shove me out there.'

Julius's frown was so deep it was like a trench between his eyes. 'You poor little kid. What about your mother? Didn't she stand up for you?'

'My mum was unable to stand up for herself, let alone me,' Holly said. 'He'd done such a good job of eroding her self-esteem, she chose death instead of life. He drove her to it. He hates me because I didn't cave in to him. That's why he keeps making trouble for me. He follows me wherever I go. He has ways and means of reminding me I can't escape. But I *will* escape. I'm determined to get away and make a new life for myself.'

Julius took both of her hands in his, holding them gently but securely. 'He can't touch you while you're with me. I'll make sure of it.'

Holly's chest swelled with hope at his implacable tone. How long had it been since she'd felt safe? Truly safe? 'Thank you…'

He touched her face with a barely there brush stroke of his bent knuckles. His eyes had a tender look that made the base of her spine hum. 'I can't imagine how difficult your life must've been compared to mine,' he said. 'No wonder you came in that first day with your fists up.'

'Yeah, well, sorry about that, but I like to get in first in case things turn out nasty, which they invariably do,' she said. 'Maybe it's my fault. I attract trouble. I can't seem to help myself. It's automatic.'

'No.' His hands took hers again in a firm but gentle hold. 'You shouldn't blame yourself. Your stepfather sounds like a creep. He belongs in jail, not you.'

Holly looked at their joined hands. Hers were so small compared to his. She slowly brought her gaze up to his. His eyes meshed with hers in a look that made her legs feel fizzy. 'Why are you looking at me like that?' she said.

'How am I looking at you?' His voice was a deep, resonant rumble.

'Like you're going to kiss me.'

He brushed an imaginary strand of hair away from her face. 'What gives you the idea I'm going to kiss you?' His mouth was half an inch from hers, his breath a warm, minty breeze against her lips.

'Just a feeling.'

His lips nudged hers in a playful manner. 'Do you always trust your feelings?'

Holly slipped her arms around his neck and pressed herself closer. 'Mostly.'

His mouth brushed hers, once, twice, three times. 'This is crazy. I shouldn't be doing this.'

'*This* being…?'

He rested his forehead against hers. 'Tell me to stop.'

'No.'

'Tell me, Holly. I *need* you to tell me.'

'I want you to kiss me,' Holly said. 'I want you to make love to me.' As soon as she said the words, she realised how much she meant them. How from the moment she'd met him she'd been drawn to him like a moth to a bright streetlight on a hot summer's night. The desire he triggered in her was unlike anything she'd ever felt before. She wanted him. She ached for him. She burned for him.

He looked at her with darkened eyes, the pupils wide with desire. 'Why?'

'Because we're attracted to each other and we might as well make the most of it.'

One of his hands cupped her face, the other rested in the small of her back. 'Why me?'

'Why not you?' she said. 'You're single. I'm single. What's the problem?'

He was still frowning. 'Is once going to be enough?'

Holly stroked the side of his jaw. 'Do you have to think about everything before you act? Don't you ever just go with the flow?'

He turned her palm towards his mouth and kissed it, all the while holding her gaze. 'Do you ever stop and think before you act?'

She shivered as his kiss travelled all the way to her core. 'I'm thinking we should make the most of the fact that Sophia's away with her sister.' Is that why he'd sent his housekeeper away? Perhaps it was unconscious on his part but he had cleared the way for them to indulge in an affair without an audience.

He framed her face with his hands, his expression darkly serious. 'I want you like I've never wanted anyone else.'

'Same.'

His head came down, and his mouth sealed hers in a kiss as hot as a flashpoint. Heat pooled between her legs as his tongue drove through the seam of her mouth to find hers. Lust raced through her blood as he stroked and thrust and cajoled her tongue into play. His body crushed hers to his, every hard contour of his enticing every softer one of hers. Her breasts peaked against his chest, her pelvis thrumming with want as she felt the thickened ridge of him.

His hands moved over her lightly, touching, exploring, discovering. He came to her breasts, lifting her top out of the way so he could access them. He swirled his tongue over and around her nipple, making her ache with longing as his teeth gently nipped and tugged at her flesh.

His hands skimmed down the sides of her body to grasp her hips, holding her tightly against the throb of his need. He made a deep sound at the back of his throat as she moved against him. A sound of approval, of want, of raw, primal lust.

'Not here,' he said as he swept her up in his arms and carried her towards his suite.

Holly noticed the balcony doors were open as she pulled him down with her on the mattress, but she pushed her fear away, not willing to be separated for a second in case he changed his mind. Her whole body was on fire. Pulsating with a longing so intense it was mind-blowing. Every part of her body was alive and sensitive. Every inch of her skin ached for his touch.

Julius must have read her mind for he began working on her clothes while she did her best to get him out of his. Her hands weren't cooperating in her haste to feel his naked skin. They were fumbling in excitement, and he had to take over. Holly watched as he unbuttoned his shirt before shrugging it off and tossing it to the floor. She put her hands on his chest, spreading her fingers over his pectoral muscles, her palms tickled by the light covering of masculine hair sprinkled over his chest.

He came down to her to caress her breasts with his lips and tongue, making her squirm and shiver with delight with every movement he made. He kissed his way from her breasts down over her stomach, dipping his tongue into the shallow cave of her belly button before going lower.

Holly sucked in a breath when he came to the heart of her. The feel of his lips separating her and the sexy rasp of his tongue against her sensitive flesh made her arch her spine like a well-pleasured cat. The ripples of an orgasm took her by surprise, taking over her body, shaking it, tossing it into a maelstrom of ecstasy that made her gasp out loud.

But even as the pleasure faded he was stirring her to new feelings, new sensations, new anticipations, as he sourced a condom and positioned himself between her thighs.

His mouth came back to hers as he entered her in a slick, deep thrust that made her whole body quake in response. His thrusts were slow and measured at first, allowing her time to get used to him. But then as she breathlessly urged him on he upped the pace, deeper, harder, faster, until she was rocking against him for that final push into paradise. He reached between their bodies to give her that extra bit of friction that pitched her over the edge. She cried out as the sensations tore through her in a rush, delicious wave upon delicious wave, roll upon roll. He waited until she was coming down from the spike before he let go. Holly felt him tense and then spill, his whole body shuddering until he finally went still.

It was a new thing for Holly to lie in a man's arms without wanting to push him off or rush off to the shower. It was a new thing for her to not feel uncomfortable with the silence. Not to have regrets over what her body had done or had had done to it by a partner. Her body was in a delicious state of lassitude, every limb feeling boneless, her mind drifting like flotsam.

After a moment Julius propped himself up on his arms to look at her. 'Am I too heavy for you?'

Holly stroked her hands down to the dip in his spine. 'No.'

He brushed a fingertip over her lower lip, his expression thoughtful. 'I might've rushed you. It's been a while.'

'You didn't,' she said. 'It was…perfect. You were perfect.'

He kissed her on the mouth softly. Lightly. 'This is usually when I say I have work to do or head to the shower.'

'Classy.'

He gave a wry smile. 'If you give me a couple of minutes, I'll be ready for round two.'

Holly arched her brows. 'So this isn't a one-off then?'

His eyes darkened as they held hers. 'Is that all you want?'

She shrugged noncommittally and looked away. 'The itch has been scratched, hasn't it?'

He took her chin between his finger and thumb and made her look at him. 'This isn't the sort of itch that can be cured with one scratch.'

Holly kept her expression screened. 'What're you suggesting? A fling? A relationship? Not sure what your family would have to say about you and me hanging out as a couple. Or the press, for that matter.'

His frown pulled at his forehead like stitches beneath the skin. 'What I do in my private life is my business, no one else's, including my family.'

'What about Sophia?'

'What about her?'

Holly tiptoed her fingers up his spine to the back of his neck where his hair was curling. 'What's she going to say when she finds out we're sleeping together?'

'We won't tell her.'

Holly laughed. 'Like that's going to work. She'll know as soon as she comes back.'

He rolled away and got off the bed to dispense with the condom, a deep frown still dividing his forehead. He picked up his trousers and stepped into them, zipping them up with unnecessary force. 'What's your caseworker going to say when you tell her about us?'

'I'm not going to tell her,' Holly said. 'Why would I? It's none of her business.'

Julius scooped his shirt and thrust his arms into the sleeves. 'We can't continue this. It's wrong. I shouldn't have allowed it to happen. I'm sorry; I take full responsibility.'

Holly swung her legs over the edge of the bed and reached for her nearest article of clothing. 'Yeah, well, I guess it was just a pity thing on your part, huh?'

'What?' His tone was sharp, shocked…annoyed.

'You only slept with me because you felt sorry for me after I told you about my crappy childhood.'

His frown was so deep his eyebrows met over the bridge of his nose. 'That's not true.'

She gave him a direct look. 'Isn't it?'

He scraped a hand through his hair. 'No. Yes. Maybe. I don't know.'

Holly finished pulling on her clothes before she came over to him. 'It's fine, Julius. Stop stressing. I'm okay with a one-off. Doesn't make sense to get too cosy, since I'll be on my way in a couple of weeks.'

He looked at her for a long, pulsing moment. 'I suppose you got what you wanted.'

She arched a brow. 'That being?'

'From the moment you stepped into this place, you had your mind set on getting me to break, didn't you?' he said. 'It was your goal. Your mission. You did everything you could to prove I couldn't resist you. Well, you were right. I couldn't.'

Holly was a little ashamed of how close to the mark he was. But what was even more concerning was how she had ended up wanting him more than she had wanted anyone. She didn't know how to handle such want. Such longing. The need was still there. It was a sated beast that would all too soon wake again and be growling, prowling for sustenance. Even now she could feel her body stirring the longer she looked into Julius's dark navy eyes with their glittering cynicism.

'What will you do now you've achieved your goal?' he said. 'Give a tell-all interview to the press?'

Holly shifted her gaze from his in case he saw how hurt she felt. 'You have serious trust issues.'

He laughed. '*I* have trust issues?'

She swung back to glare at him. 'Do you really think I would share my body with you and then tell everyone about it? I'd be hurting myself more than you.'

'They pay big money for scandalous stories. Big money. You could set yourself up on this.'

Holly pressed her lips together as she went in hunt of her shoes but she could only find one. Frustration and hurt tangled in a tight knot in her chest, making it hard for her to breathe. She had given him every reason to think she would sell out to score points against him. The shaming truth was a few days ago she might well have done it. But something had changed. *She* had changed. His touch, his concern, his promise of protection had made something inside her shift. She couldn't find a way to reassemble herself. It was as if the puzzle pieces of her personality had been scattered and she didn't know how to get them back into order. The things she had wanted before were not what she wanted now.

It was disturbing—terrifying—to allow her nascent hopes and dreams to get a foothold. For the first time in her life, she'd caught a glimpse of what it would be like to be secure in a relationship. To be with a man who looked out for her, who wanted the best for her, who would help her reach her potential instead of sabotaging it. To be honoured and cherished. To be celebrated instead of ridiculed. To be accepted.

To be trusted.

To be loved.

Holly took a scalding breath and forced herself to look at him. 'I guess you'd better call Natalia and get her to take me away, then.'

Something passed over his features. 'No.'

'Why not?' Holly said, trying to squash the bubble of hope that bloomed in her chest. 'I'm nothing but trouble. I belong in jail, or so you said the other day.'

He let out a long breath and came back to where she was standing. He put his hands on her hunched shoulders, his touch as light as goose down but as hot as fire. 'You're not going anywhere.'

She ran the point of her tongue out over her paper-dry lips. 'I wouldn't have done it. I wouldn't have called the press.'

He gave her shoulders a light squeeze. 'I'm sorry.'

'It's okay. I get that you want to keep your privacy secure,' Holly said. 'I haven't exactly given you the impression I'm someone you could trust.'

He tipped up her chin with the tip of his finger. 'What am I going to do with you, Holly Perez?'

Holly looked into his sapphire-blue gaze. 'You could start by kissing me.'

He pressed a soft kiss to her mouth. 'Then what?'

She tilted her head as if thinking about it. 'You could put your hand on my breast.'

He cupped her breast through her clothes, his eyes glinting. 'And then what?'

She moved closer, letting her breath mingle with his as she slipped her hands around his neck. 'Figure it out,' she said, and his mouth came down and sealed hers.

CHAPTER TEN

A FEW DAYS later Holly watched as Julius slept. He was a quiet sleeper, not restless and fidgety like her. She could have watched him for hours, memorising his features, storing them in her mind for the time when she would be gone from his life. She had been playing a game of pretend with herself over the past few days, a silly little game where she wouldn't have to leave at the end of the time she had left.

She had even been so foolish as to picture her and Julius building a life together. Having a family together. Building a future together. Things she had never allowed herself to dream of before. She hadn't even realised she wanted those things until now. Every day she spent in his company she found herself wanting him more. Not just physically, although that had only got better and better. It was more of an intellectual connection, one she had never felt with anyone else. He inspired her, excited her, and challenged her.

Holly traced one of his eyebrows with her fingertip. 'Are you awake?'

'No.'

She smiled and traced the other eyebrow. That was the other thing she liked about him—he had a sense of humour underneath all that gruff starchiness. 'Are you dreaming?' she said.

'Yes, of this hot girl who's in my bed touching me with her clever little hands.'

Holly reached down and stroked his swollen length. 'Like this?'

'Mmm, just like that.'

'And in this dream did that same girl slide down your body like this?' She moved down his body, letting her breasts touch him from chest to groin.

'That's it,' he said in a low growl. 'I never want to wake up.'

She sent her tongue down the length of his shaft, then swirled it over the head and around the sensitive glans.

'Condom, *querida.*'

'I want to taste you.'

He muttered an expletive as she opened her mouth over him, drawing on him until he was breathing heavily. 'You don't have to…'

'I want to,' Holly said. 'You do it to me. Why shouldn't I do it to you?'

'I've never had someone do it in the raw before.'

'Lucky me to be the first.'

He frowned for a moment but it soon disappeared as Holly got to business. She watched him as she drew on him, her own excitement building as she saw the effect she was having on him. He pulled out just as he spilled, the erotic pumping of his essence thrilling her in a way she hadn't expected.

He threaded his fingers through her hair in long, soothing strokes that made her scalp tingle in delight. 'Holly…'

She looked up from where she had been resting her cheek against his stomach. 'What?'

He had one of his deep-in-thought frowns on his forehead. After a moment the frown relaxed as he smiled faintly. 'Just... Holly.'

She stroked his stubbly jaw. 'Not getting all sentimental on me, are you?'

The frown was back. 'What do you mean?'

Holly propped herself on one elbow as she trailed her fingers up and down his chest. 'This is just for now. Us, I mean. I'm going to England once I'm done here.'

He pushed her hand away and got off the bed. 'I know you are. I'm glad you are. It's the right thing to do.' He pulled on a bathrobe and tied the belt, his expression shuttered.

'You don't sound very happy about it.'

He threw her an irritated look. 'Why wouldn't I be happy about it?'

She gave a shrug. 'Thought you might miss me.'

'I will but that doesn't mean I want you to stay.'

Holly sat up and pulled her knees into her chest. 'I wouldn't stay if you asked me.'

'I'm not going to ask you.'

'Fine. Glad we got that settled.'

He went to the balcony doors and unlocked them. Holly stiffened. 'What are you doing?'

'I want some fresh air.'

Bitterness burned in her gullet. 'You're only doing that to get rid of me. It's cruel, Julius. You know how much it freaks me out. I thought you understood. I'll only come in here if those doors are closed.'

'It's just a balcony, for God's sake.'

Tears sprouted but Holly tried to blink them back.

'It's not just a bloody balcony!' She got off the bed, pulling the sheet with her to cover herself. 'I spent hours and hours—years—of my life frightened out of my wits, and now you're using that fear, *exploiting* that fear, to push me away because you're scared of how you feel about me leaving.'

He flung the doors wide open and stepped out on to the balcony, standing with his back to her as he looked out over the estate.

Holly felt a gnarled knot of emotion clog her throat. Her heart was beating too fast, too erratically. Her skin was icy-cold and then clammy-hot. Her vision blurred with tears. She tried to get away but the sheet wrapped around her halted her progress. She tripped, stumbled and then fell in an ungainly heap on the floor.

'Are you all right?' Julius was by her side in seconds.

Holly batted his hand away. 'No, of course I'm not all right. Close the freaking doors, will you?'

He gripped her chin between his finger and thumb. 'You're fine, Holly. Look at me. You're fine. No one's going to hurt you.'

She glared at him. 'You hurt me. You did. You shouldn't have done that.' Tears leaked out of her eyes in spite of all she did to try and stop them. She landed a punch on his arm but it glanced off as if she had hit stone. 'You sh-shouldn't have done that.'

'Hey…hey…hey…' He drew her against him, resting his chin on top of her head as he gently stroked her back in soothing circles. 'It's all right, *querida*. I'm sorry. I shouldn't have done it. I'm sorry. Shh, don't cry.'

'I'm not c-crying.'

'Of course you're not.' He kept stroking her, holding her.

'I'm angry, that's all.'

'Of course you are. You have every right to be. I was being a jerk.'

'If you want me to leave the room or get out of your life just say so, okay?' she said against his chest. 'I can take a hint. I'm not stupid.'

There was a deep silence.

Holly listened to the sound of his breathing. Felt the steady rise and fall of his chest against her cheek and the slow beat of his heart. Felt his hand gently stroking her hair, his chin resting on top of her head. Felt her heart squeeze at the thought of how soon this was going to end.

Before she knew it, she would be on her way to a new life in England. The only contact she would have with him would be seeing articles about his family in the press. She wasn't falling in love with him. She wasn't. It was just that he was so...so different from all the men she had met in the past. He was impossibly strong, yet tender when he needed to be. He was a control freak but that showed he had discipline and self-control. He was a man with honour and standards. No one had ever taken the time to get to know her like he had done. He was interested in what made her the person she was and he inspired her to become who she was meant to be.

How could she not feel a little regret over her imminent departure? It was normal. It didn't mean she was falling in love with him. She had never been in love before and didn't intend to be now. She had seen first-hand the damage loving someone could do. You lost your power, your autonomy, your self-respect and your freedom. Love was a trap. A cage that, once you were in, you couldn't get out of. That wasn't what she had planned for her life.

Julius eased back to look down at her. 'I want you to do something for me.'

'What?'

He took her by the hands in a gentle hold. 'I want you to come out on the balcony with me.'

Holly tried to pull away but his grip tightened. 'No. *No*. Don't ask me to do that. I won't. I can't.'

He kept her imprisoned hands close to his chest. 'I'll be with you the whole time. I won't let go of you. Trust me, Holly.'

She felt the panic rise in her chest. Felt the bookcase flatten her lungs until she could barely inflate them enough to breathe. Could she do it? Could she trust him to stand by her and hold her, to help her confront her worst nightmare? Her skin crawled with dread. Her heart raced. Her stomach churned. 'I—I'm not sure I can do it… My stepfather used to drag me out there by the hair. He would lock me out there and then beat up my mum while I watched. Don't make me do it. I c-can't.'

Julius's expression flinched as she spoke but he kept hold of her hands, holding her gaze as he kissed her clenched knuckles one by one. 'Don't let him win any longer, *querida*. All this time he's had it over you by controlling you with fear. Give your fear to me. Trust me. I won't let you fall.'

I think I'm already falling, Holly thought. Feelings she had never expected to feel for anyone were slipping past the barriers she had erected around her heart. Her defences were no match for his tenderness, his concern, his steadiness and support. She couldn't allow herself to fall for him. This was a temporary arrangement that would end once her community service was over. She was a fool to imagine any other outcome. He was from a completely different world. He would have no place for her in it. She didn't belong. She was an outcast. A misfit. A nobody that nobody wanted.

'Okay…' Her voice came out scratchy as it squeezed past the strangulation of her fear.

He led her to the balcony doors. 'Okay so far?'

She nodded, swallowing another wave of panic. He opened the doors, and the fresh air wafted over her face. She gripped his hand so tightly she wondered why he didn't wince in pain.

'Good girl,' he said. 'Now, take one step at a time. We'll stop if it gets too much. It's your call.'

Holly took one step onto the balcony on legs as unsteady as a new-born foal's. The smell of freshly mown grass drifted past her nostrils. She tried to concentrate on the view, hoping it would distract her from thinking about the fear that chilled her to the bone.

'You're doing so well,' he said. 'Want to try a couple more steps?'

She took another thorny breath and moved one step forward. His hands squeezed hers in encouragement. She looked up at him and gave him a wobbly smile. 'Nice view from up here.'

'Yes,' he said but she noticed he wasn't looking at the view.

Holly looked at their joined hands. He wasn't letting her go. He wasn't pushing her beyond her limits. He had held true to his promise. The weight of fear began to lift off her chest. She could breathe. She could feel her heart rate gradually slowing. She wasn't cured by any means but she had made progress. She hadn't been anywhere near a balcony since she'd been a teenager. Years of terror had stalked her. Controlled her. She had taken two steps forward into a future without fear. Two steps. It wasn't much but it was enough to give her a glimmer of hope.

Holly looked up into his deep-blue gaze. 'Thank you...'

'I haven't done anything,' he said. 'I was just holding your hand. Next time will be easier. Soon you'll be doing it all by yourself.'

'I'm not so sure about that,' she said with a little shudder.

'You underestimate yourself,' he said. 'You can do anything if you try. You have so much potential. Don't let anyone take it away from you.'

Holly pulled away to go back inside. She hugged her elbows with her hands crossed over. It was all very well for him to talk about potential. He'd had a good education. Family money and opportunities she could only dream about. He might find his parents difficult but at least he had them.

She had no one.

Julius came up behind her and put his hands on her shoulders. 'Would you like to go out to dinner?'

Holly turned to look at him with a frown. 'In public?'

'That's where the restaurants tend to be.'

'Yes, and so are people with camera phones.'

'I know a quiet little place where we won't be disturbed,' he said. 'I know the guy who runs it. He'll let us have a private room.'

Holly hadn't quite let her frown go. 'Why are you doing this?'

'Doing what?'

'Acting like this is a normal relationship.'

A muscle moved near his mouth. 'You deserve a break from cooking, surely?'

'Then order takeaway.'

'It's just dinner,' he said. 'I sometimes take Sophia out for a meal.'

'I'd rather not.'

'Why not? You have the clothes to wear.'

Holly unwrapped her body from the sheet she was wearing and reached for a bathrobe. 'I'm happy to sleep with you, okay? But don't ask me to act like we're a proper couple. Date nights are out of the question.'

'Fine,' he said casually but it didn't fool her for a second. 'Forget I asked.'

Holly bit down on her lip as he strode into the en suite. He was upset with her for refusing but what else could she do? Dinner would have been nice but how could she control her emotions if he pressed her to do couple stuff? A romantic dinner for two was just plain wrong. She was not his romantic partner.

She never would be.

Julius knew he had no right to feel annoyed Holly had refused to go out in public with him. He knew they weren't in a relationship. It was just a fling. A convenient interlude that was going to end once her community service was up. He should, in principle, be in agreement about keeping their affair out of the public eye but he had wanted to spend time with her away from the villa where she felt like a member of his staff rather than his equal. He wanted them to be just two ordinary people who had an attraction for each other. He wanted to spoil her in a way she had never been spoilt before.

The very fact she didn't want to go public about their

involvement was a confirmation of the sort of person she was underneath all that 'junkyard dog' bluster. She was sensitive and easily hurt. She hid that vulnerability behind her don't-mess-with-me façade. The horror of her past sickened him. He wanted to make it up to her. To make her feel safe in a way she had never felt before. He needed time to do that. But how much time did he have? Not much. Not enough.

For some reason every time he thought of her leaving he got a pain below his ribs. A tight, cramping pain as if someone was jabbing him. What would happen to her when she went to England? She had no one. No family to watch out for her. She would be totally alone. His family annoyed the hell out of him most of the time but at least he knew they were there when he needed them. Who would Holly turn to if things went sour?

The way she had trusted him to take her out on the balcony had moved him deeply. He had seen the years of terror in her face. Felt it in her hands as they gripped his so tightly. And yet she had stood out there in his arms and given him a shaky smile, *trusting* him to keep her safe. Who would keep her safe once she left him?

Why the heck was he ruminating so much about her leaving? Of course she had to leave. It was what she wanted. A new start in her mother's homeland. A chance to get her life back on track, to pursue her dreams and put her past behind her. A past Julius would be part of. Would she ever think of him? Miss him?

He gave himself a mental shake and tried to refocus on the programme code in front of him. He wasn't supposed to be developing feelings for her. It was fine to care about someone, sure. It was fine to want to see her get on her feet and reach her potential. But caring so much he couldn't bear to think of letting her go was ridiculous. He hadn't wanted her to come here in the first place. How could he possibly want her to stay indefinitely?

He didn't do indefinitely.

Julius's mobile rang, and he was about to ignore it but changed his mind when he saw it was his sister, Miranda. Finally. 'Nice of you to get back to me.'

'I'm sorry but I didn't feel like talking to anyone,' Miranda said.

It was what his baby sister did when things got difficult. She went to ground. He knew she would call him eventually but it worried him she had left it so long. 'You okay?'

'God, it's just so embarrassing,' she said. 'Mum is beside herself and for once I can't blame her.'

'Have you met the girl yet?'

'No,' Miranda said. 'Dad's pushing for it. He wants a big family reunion. Can you believe it? Talk about lack of sensitivity. I just want to run away and hide some place until it all blows over.'

'Have the press hassled you for a comment?'

'Like, every day,' she said. 'The worse thing is they keep making comparisons. I'm now officially known as the ugly sister.'

'That's rubbish and you know it,' Julius said.

'Have you seen her, Julius?' Miranda asked. 'She's stunning. Like one of those lingerie supermodels. And guess what? She's an aspiring actor. Dad is so proud he finally produced a child with theatrical ambition. He keeps going on and on about it. It's nauseating.'

'What's she been in? I haven't heard of her before now.'

'She's only been in amateur things but now all she'll

have to do is name drop and the red carpet will be rolled
out for her. You wait and see.'

'Connections will only get her so far,' Julius said.
'She'll need talent.'

Miranda gave a gusty sigh. 'I don't want to talk about
it any more. So, how are you?'

'Fine. Been busy working.'

'Same old.'

He gave a rueful smile. 'Same old.'

'When are you coming over?' she said. 'Have you
got any plans to visit?'

'Not right now.'

There was a short silence.

'Are you dating someone?' Miranda asked.

Julius tossed the question back even though he already knew the answer. 'Are you?'

'I know you think I'm wasting my life but I loved
Mark,' Miranda said in her stock-standard defensive
tone she used whenever the topic of her moving on with
her life was brought up.

'I know you did, sweetheart,' Julius said gently. 'And
he loved you. But if things were the other way around
I reckon he would've moved on by now.'

'You obviously haven't been in love,' Miranda said.
'You don't know what it's like to lose the only person
in the world you want to be with.'

Julius felt that sudden pang beneath his ribs again. He
was going to lose Holly. In a matter of days, she would
be gone. He would never see her again.

Which was how it should be, as she had a right to
move on with her new life without him interfering.

Julius put his phone down after he'd finished listening to his little sister tell him a thousand reasons why

she would never date another man. He let out a long sigh. There were times when he wondered if love was worth all the heartache. So far he had avoided it.

So far...

CHAPTER ELEVEN

A COUPLE OF days later Julius finished a tele-conference that had taken longer than he'd expected and went in search of Holly. She was out by the pool scooping out leaves with the net. 'One of the groundsmen can do that,' he said.

She turned around and smiled one of her cheeky smiles. 'Have you got something you'd rather me do indoors?'

He put his arms around her, bringing her bikini-clad body against his fully clothed one. 'Why are you always wandering around the place half-dressed?' he growled at her playfully.

'All the better to tempt you, my dear,' she said.

Julius brought his mouth down to hers. The heat of their mouths meeting always surprised him. Delighted him. She didn't kiss in half-measures. She kissed with her whole body. He drew her closer, his body responding to the slim, sun-kissed contours of hers. He kept on kissing her as he unhooked her bikini top so he could access her breasts. Her hands went to the buttons of his shirt, undoing each one with spine-tingling purpose.

He put his mouth to her breast, sucking, licking and teasing the engorged flesh until she was making breathless little sounds of need. He untied the strings of her bikini bottoms and cupped the pert curves of her bottom in his hands.

She tilted her head back to look at him. 'This is a little unfair. I'm completely naked and you're fully dressed.'

Julius swept his tongue over her pouting bottom lip. 'Let's take this indoors.'

She rubbed against him sensuously. 'Why not have a swim with me first?'

He couldn't resist her in this mood. She was so damn sexy he could barely hold himself in check. Within seconds he, too, had stripped off—apart from a quickly sheathed condom—and was in the pool with her, holding her against his aroused body as she smiled up at him with those dancing, caramel-brown eyes. He lowered his mouth to hers, his senses reeling as her tongue came into play with his. Her hands were around his waist, then caressing his chest, then going even lower to hold him until he was ready to explode. The water only heightened the sensations. The silky cool of it against their heated bodies made him all the more frantic for release.

He walked her backwards until she was up against the edge of the pool but, rather than have her back marked by the pool's edge, he turned her so her back was against the front of his body. He kissed his way from her earlobe to her neck and back again, trailing his tongue over her scented flesh, wondering how he was going to stop himself coming ahead of schedule with her bottom pressed up against his erection. She made a sound of encouragement, part whimper, part gasp, as he moved between legs.

He entered her deeply, barely able to control himself as her hot, wet body gripped him like a clamp. He kept thrusting, building a pace that had her hands gripping the edge of the pool for balance. He felt every delicious ripple of her inner flesh, the contraction of her around him as she came, triggering his own mind-blowing release.

He didn't want to move. He wanted to stand there on his still shaking legs and hold her against him.

She turned in his arms, looking up at him with a face glowing with the aftermath of pleasure. 'Ever done it in the pool before?'

'No.'

'Lucky me to be your first pool—'

Julius put his fingertip over her mouth to stop her saying the crude word he suspected she was going to say. 'Don't.'

She pushed his hand away. 'Don't be so squeamish, Julius. It's just sex.'

Just sex.

Was it? Was it just sex for him? Maybe for her it was but for him it didn't feel anything like the sex he'd had in the past. His whole body felt different with her. *He* felt different. Not just in his flesh but in his mind. Sex had gone from being a purely physical experience to a more cerebral—dared he admit it?—emotional one. He liked having Holly around. She was funny and playful, exciting and daring in a way that made him shift out of his comfort zone. But he had helped her out of her comfort zone, too. She had even allowed the balcony doors to be open in his suite when they made love the past few nights.

Made love.

The words jolted him. Maybe it wasn't 'just sex' after all. He made love to her. His body worshipped hers, pleasured hers and delighted in giving as well as receiving it. He had never wanted a woman more than her. She made him feel aroused by just looking at him. The scent of her was enough to make him hard. He only had to walk into a room she had been in earlier and his blood would be pumping. Her touch made his flesh tingle all over. The dancing tiptoe movements of her fingers made his pulse thunder and his heart race. Everything about her turned him on. He couldn't imagine another woman being as thrilling and satisfying as her.

But she was leaving in four days...

Which was fine. Just fine. She had her plans. He had his. He wasn't after anything serious. They'd had their fun. And it had been fun, much more fun than he'd realised a fling could be. She had taught him to loosen up. He had helped her confront her fears. She had revealed her past to him, which he hoped meant she was ready to move on from it. He wanted her to succeed. She had so much going for her. Her energy, passion and drive were wonderful qualities if channelled in the right direction.

Holly linked her arms around his neck. 'What's that big, old sober frown for?'

Julius forced a smile. 'Was I frowning?'

She put her fingertip between his brows. 'You get this deep ridge right here when you're thinking.'

He captured her finger and trailed his tongue the length of it. 'I'm thinking it might be good to go inside before we both get burned to a crisp.'

'Good point,' she said and walked up the steps of the pool.

Julius stood spellbound as she emerged from the

water like a nymph. She draped her wet hair over one shoulder as she squeezed the water out, reminding him of a mermaid. Her creamy skin was lightly tanned in spite of the sunscreen he'd seen her using. Her body was fit and toned yet utterly, irresistibly feminine.

She stepped into her bikini bottoms and tied the strings before she went in search of her top. Her smooth brow suddenly creased. 'Is that a car?' she asked, hurriedly covering herself.

Julius had been too focussed on her delectable body even to register anything but how gorgeous she looked. But now he could hear the scrabble of tyres over the gravel of the driveway.

'Are you expecting anyone?' Holly asked.

He vaulted out of the pool and reached for his trousers, not even stopping to dry himself. 'No,' he said. 'No one can get through the gates without the security code, unless it's one of the gardeners coming back in after mowing out front.'

'That doesn't sound like a ride-on mower,' she said, speaking Julius's thoughts out loud.

He shrugged on his shirt and quickly buttoned it. Under normal circumstances he would have got Sophia to answer the door. But with his housekeeper still away with her sister he could hardly send Holly dressed in nothing but a bikini. 'I'll see who it is,' he said. 'You stay here.'

Julius's heart sank when he saw the chauffeur-driven black limousine pull up in front of the villa. His mother. Dressed to the nines. There was no press entourage that he could see but he knew it wouldn't be long. His mother didn't go anywhere without the press documenting her every move.

'I'm coming to stay, Julius,' she said as her driver helped her alight from the car as if she were stepping out on the red carpet. 'I had to get away. The press haven't left me alone for a minute.'

'Have they followed you here?' he said.

'Not that I know of,' Elisabetta said. 'Why are you frowning? Aren't you pleased to see me? I cancelled the rest of my season on Broadway to spend time with you. This is the only place I'll be left alone. I was going to stay with Jake but he's always got some girl coming and going. And Miranda refuses to get involved. Not that I'd want to stay in her poky little flat.'

'Look, now's not a good time,' Julius said.

Elisabetta pouted. 'Don't give me your stupid work excuse. Your work can wait for your mother, surely? Don't you realise how desperate I am? Your father's ruined everything.' She paused long enough to narrow her gaze at him. 'Why are you all wet? And your shirt is buttoned up the wrong way.'

Julius gave himself a mental kick. 'I was having… er…a quick dip. You caught me by surprise.'

Elisabetta continued her tirade. 'I'm *so* furious. Do you know the girl's mother was a housemaid at the hotel he was staying in? A housemaid! How could he be so pathetic?'

Julius pushed back his wet hair with his hand. 'I really don't have time for this right now.'

'You never have time,' Elisabetta said, flouncing up the steps. 'All you have time for is work.'

'Mother, you can't stay,' Julius said. 'It's not…convenient. My housekeeper's away for a few days and I'm not prepared for visitors.'

Elisabetta turned with a theatrical swish of her designer skirt. 'Why do you always push me away? Can't you see I need you to support me right now?'

'I understand things are awful for you just now but you can't just dump yourself here without giving me notice,' Julius said. 'You could've at least called or texted first.'

Elisabetta's gaze narrowed again. 'Have you got someone with you? A lover? Who is it? You're such a dark horse. You never tell me anything. Even the press never knows what you're up to—unlike your brother.'

How could he explain his relationship with Holly to his mother? How could he explain it to himself? Was it even a relationship? Wasn't it just a fling? A temporary thing they both knew would come to an end at the end of the week? 'I like to keep my private life out of the news,' Julius said. 'Which is why you coming here is such a problem for me. You're a press magnet.'

'I hope you're not going to suddenly take your father's side in this,' Elisabetta said as if she hadn't heard a word he'd said.

'Why would I do that?' Julius said. 'What he did was unconscionable.'

'I blame that tramp who seduced him,' his mother said as she entered the front door of the villa. 'She betrayed him by not having the abortion he paid for. At least he offered to sort things out for her but what did she do? Went ahead and had the brat. The decent thing would've been to get rid of the mistake. Pretend it never happened. But no. Those ghastly little gold-diggers are all the same.'

His mother's logic—if he could call it that—had always been hard to follow. He was pretty certain Katherine Winwood would not like to be referred to as a 'mistake' or hear her deceased mother referred to as a 'ghastly little gold-digger'.

'If Kat's mother was such a gold-digger why did she wait until she was on her death bed to reveal her daughter's paternity?' he asked. 'Why not come forward years ago and line her pockets with silence money?'

Elisabetta threw him a fulminating look. 'How can you *defend* her? She was a housemaid, for God's sake.'

Just then Holly appeared dressed neatly in a skirt and blouse with her still-damp hair scraped back in a neat chignon. 'Welcome, Ms Albertini,' she said. 'Would you like me to take your things upstairs to your room?'

Elisabetta gave Holly an assessing look before turning to Julius. 'I thought you said your housekeeper was away?'

'She is,' he said. 'Holly's filling in for her.'

Elisabetta looked at Holly and then back at Julius, her expression tightening. 'So that's how it is, is it? You're sleeping with the hired help. Just like your father.'

Julius clenched his jaw. 'I won't have you insult Holly.'

His mother glared at Holly. 'I suppose you think you've got yourself a meal ticket by seducing my son.'

Holly hitched up her chin, her stance one of cool dignity. 'Would you like a drink brought up to your room? A bite to eat? Some fresh fruit?'

Elisabetta flattened her mouth. 'Did you hear what I said?'

'Yes, Ms Albertini, but I chose to ignore it on account of you being travel weary and upset over recent events,' Holly said. 'Now, if you'd like a drink or some other refreshment, I'll see to it, otherwise I'll leave Julius to show you to your room.'

His mother's brown eyes flashed as she turned to

Julius. 'Did you hear how she spoke to me? Get rid of her. Get her out of my sight. I won't be patronised as if I'm a child!'

'Then don't act like one,' Julius said. 'Holly might be acting as my housekeeper but that doesn't mean she isn't entitled to respect.'

'It's fine, Julius,' Holly chipped in. 'I can handle snobs like your mother.'

Elisabetta bristled. Her lips were pursed, her eyes blazing, her hands clenched. 'You disgusting little sow,' she threw at Holly. 'He can have anyone he wants. Why would he want *you*?'

'I'm great in bed,' Holly said. 'Plus, I cook an awesome meal. Oh, and did I mention I give great—?'

'That's enough,' Julius cut in quickly. 'Mother, you need to leave. Find a hotel somewhere. This is not the place for you right now.'

Elisabetta narrowed her eyes to slits. 'You'd choose *her* over your own mother? What sort of son are you? Anyone with eyes could see she's nothing but trailer trash.'

'Takes one to know one,' Holly said, calmly inspecting her cuticles.

Elisabetta's eyes bulged in outrage. 'What did you say?'

'Right. Time to go.' Julius took his mother's arm and led her back to the waiting car. His mother didn't like being reminded of her poverty-stricken background. It was mostly a well-kept secret, how she had grown up on the back streets of Florence, child of a single mother who had turned tricks to put food on the table. Elisabetta had reinvented herself when she'd moved to London to find a modelling job, which had then led to acting. Julius had never met his grandmother even though she had died three years after he and Jake were born. Not because he had been told of his grandmother's death. He had by chance come across the death certificate when he'd been a teenager sorting out things in the library down at Ravensdene. It was as if Elisabetta's past hadn't existed. It was erased from her memory.

But now, having got to know a little about Holly's desolate background, he wondered if his mother had had good reason to distance herself from it. Perhaps the memories, like Holly's, were too painful. Perhaps it wasn't a matter of pride and arrogance on his mother's part but shame. Was that why Elisabetta found it hard to be a mother herself? She hadn't been nurtured in the way most loving mothers nurtured their children. Elisabetta had pushed her children away unless she'd needed them to do something for her.

Like now, for instance. His mother would never come to visit him unless she'd wanted the visit to be all about her. She had never shown any interest in his work. He suspected she barely knew anything about his career. She had certainly never asked. He had always felt resentful towards her for her lack of interest but he wondered now if that was just the way life had shaped her.

Elisabetta got back in the car with a haughty flick of her Hermes scarf. 'I wouldn't demean myself by staying under the same roof as someone as common as that little tart. She'll bring you nothing but trouble. You mark my words.'

Julius closed the door and stepped back. 'I'll call you in a couple of days. Take care of yourself.'

His mother tightened her mouth as she looked straight

ahead. 'Drive me back to the airport,' she told the driver. 'It seems I'm not welcome here.'

Holly came down the steps to join him as he watched his mother's car disappear down the driveway. 'I might've overstepped the mark…just a little,' she said.

Julius put an arm around her shoulders and brought her close to him, kissing the top of her head. 'Only a little.'

She clasped his hand around her shoulder as she watched the dust stirred up by the car finally settle. 'Why did you defend me like that, anyway?'

He turned her in his arms to look at her. 'Why wouldn't I defend you? She was being rude and disrespectful.'

Holly's mouth twisted. 'No one's ever done that for me, or at least, not for a long time.'

Julius squeezed the tops of her shoulders. 'Then it's about time somebody did.'

Her eyes flicked away from his. 'It's nice of you and all that, but I'd hate for you to be estranged from your mother just because of me. It's not like I'm even going to be here much longer.'

Julius hated being reminded of the timeline. It was getting closer and closer to the end, and he knew he had to face it, but it was like facing a yawning chasm. Once Holly left, his life would go back to normal. Normal and ordered and…empty. 'What if you stayed a little longer?'

Her gaze was suddenly wary. Guarded. 'Why would I want to do that?'

Why indeed? he thought with a stab of disappointment. Clearly he was the one with the larger emotional investment in their relationship. *Emotional investment?* What the hell did that even mean? He wasn't in love with her. Was he? No. Of course he wasn't. He just had feelings for her. Feelings that were about care and concern for her welfare. Affection. She was a sweet girl underneath that façade. He'd come to respect her. To admire her. He'd come to enjoy their relationship.

Why was he persisting in calling it a relationship? It was a fling...wasn't it? Why had he been so convinced she was developing feelings for him? He'd fooled himself their love-making had made her fall in love with him. But sex was just sex for her. Hadn't she told him that repeatedly? The ironic thing was he'd said the same thing to women he'd dated in the past.

Julius shrugged. 'Just thought you might like to come out to the desert with me.'

Her brow wrinkled like crushed silk. 'The...*desert*?'

'I'm going on a trip to check on the software in the Atacama Desert,' he said. 'It's the highest and driest desert on the planet—that's why we do the infrared astronomy there, because of the absence of water vapour. I thought you might like to come with me.'

She pulled half of her bottom lip inside her mouth before releasing it. 'Look, it's a really nice offer, but I've already booked my air fare and I don't want to be charged a rebooking fee.'

'Don't worry about the money. I can help you with that.'

Her eyes met his with the kind of implacability and pride he had come to associate with her. And admire. 'It's not about the money. I've made up my mind, Julius. I'm leaving at the end of the week. I've waited years for this. You can't ask me to change my plans just because you want to have another week or two of sex.'

'It's not about the sex, damn it,' Julius said.

Her chin came up. 'Then what is it about?'

He framed her face in his hands. He felt as if he was stepping into mid-air off a vertiginous cliff. His stomach was pitching. Her eyes were giving nothing away but he could see a tiny muscle near her mouth moving like a pulse. 'It's about you. About wanting to be with you. Not because of the sex, although that's great. The best, in fact. But because I like you.'

Her eyes took on a cynical sheen. 'You *like* me.' She didn't frame it as a surprised question or a delighted statement. It sounded like she was mocking him for using such a trite word.

Julius brushed his thumbs over her creamy cheeks. 'I like how you make me feel.'

'How do I make you feel?' Her voice was toneless. As if she didn't really care how he answered.

'You make me feel alive.'

'Just…alive?' Was that a hint of delight he was hearing in her voice? Was that a sparkle of hope shining in her toffee-brown eyes?

Julius stepped off the cliff. He could no longer deny what he felt. 'I think I'm falling in love with you. No, strike that—I *am* in love with you. There's no thinking required. I know.'

Her eyes widened to the size of billiard balls. 'You're joking.'

'I'm not joking.'

'You're mad.'

'Mad? No. Madly in love? Yes.'

She opened and closed her mouth. Swallowed. 'But… but *why*?'

'Why?' Julius asked on the tail end of a laugh. 'Because you're the most fascinating, adorable, complicated and yet sweetest person I've ever met.'

Her forehead was lined again with worry. 'But your mother hates me.'

He smoothed away her frown. 'Only because she doesn't know you yet. She'll fall for you like I did once she gets to know how wonderful you are.'

She kept pulling at her lower lip with her teeth. 'Look, I really like you, Julius, but love? I'm not sure I even know what that word means.'

Julius tried not to be put off by her lack of enthusiasm. He understood her caution. She was used to people letting her down, exploiting her. She would be the last person to speak her feelings first. She would have to feel totally secure, trust that her heart was not going to be destroyed by someone who wasn't genuine. He could live with that. He loved her enough to be patient. He didn't need the words. He needed the action. The evidence. 'Love means wanting the best for someone,' he said. 'I want the best for you, *querida*. I want you to be happy. To feel safe and secure and loved.'

Her frown was back. 'I can't feel safe. Not here. Not in Argentina.'

'Because of your stepfather?'

She held her arms against her body, visibly shrinking her frame, as if trying to contain every bit of herself into the smallest package possible. 'You don't know the power he has. The reach he has. If he knew we were involved it could get ugly. Really ugly.'

'I can handle bullies like your stepfather,' Julius said. 'I survived English boarding school, after all!'

Her eyes showed her doubts in long, dark shadows

that went all the way back to her childhood. Julius could see the fear. He could sense it. It was like a presence.

She suddenly unpeeled her arm from around her body and held it wrist-up. 'This is what my stepfather did,' she said. 'He broke my arm in four places. He told me to lie to the doctors at the hospital or he would kill my mother or me or both.'

Julius looked at the white scar on her wrist, his gut boiling with rage at what she had suffered. 'The man is a criminal,' he said. 'He needs to be charged. He needs to be locked up and the key thrown away.'

Holly laughed but it wasn't with humour. It bordered on hysteria. 'He has friends in such high places he could wriggle his way out of any charge. He's done it numerous times. I know he's out there waiting for a chance to hurt me. I'm surprised he hasn't tracked me down yet. It's unusually slow for him.'

He took her in his arms and held her close. 'I won't let him hurt you,' he said. 'I won't let anyone hurt you.'

She pressed her cheek against his chest. 'You're the nicest man I've ever met.' Her voice was so soft he had to strain his ears to hear her. 'If I was going to fall in love it would be with someone like you.'

Julius rested his chin on top of her head, holding her in the circle of his arms. He swore he would do everything he could to make her feel safe. He would not settle until he had achieved that for her. Whatever it took, he would do.

Whatever it took.

CHAPTER TWELVE

HOLLY WOKE WELL before Julius the next morning. But then, she hadn't really been asleep. Even though Julius had made love to her with exquisite tenderness and had made her feel treasured and cherished, she had lain awake most of the night with a gnawing sense of unease. Sophia was returning today after extending her break with her sister. But it wasn't just about the housekeeper finding out about Holly's relationship with Julius. It was a sense the world outside—the world she had been pretending didn't exist—was coming for her. To seek her out. To make her pay the price for the bubble of happiness she had been in.

The fact that Julius had told her he loved her should have made her feel the most blessed person in the world but instead it made her feel the opposite. It was like tempting fate. Whenever things were going well for her, something always happened to ruin it. It was the script of her life. She had no control over it. She didn't dare to be happy. Happiness was for other people—for lucky people who didn't have horrible backgrounds they couldn't escape from.

Holly slipped out of bed and padded across the room, quietly opening the balcony doors and stepping outside.

It still amazed her how Julius had helped her overcome her crippling fear. But he was right. She had allowed her stepfather to control her through fear. She stood on the balcony and breathed in the fresh morning air. The sun was just peeping over the horizon, the red and gold and crimson streaks heralding a warm day ahead.

Julius's phone beeped on the bedside table, and Holly heard him grunt as he reached out to pick it up. She turned to look at him, all sexily tousled from a deep sleep after satisfying sex. He pushed his hair back off his forehead as he read the message. She saw his face blanch. Watched as his throat moved up and down in a convulsive swallow.

She stepped back into the room, pushing away the gauzy curtain that clung to her on the way past. 'What's wrong?'

He clicked off the phone but she noticed he didn't put it back on the bedside table. He was gripping it in his hand so tightly, she was sure the screen would crack. Every knuckle on his hand was white with tension. 'Nothing.'

Holly came over to him and sat on the edge of the bed beside him. 'It can't be nothing. You look like you just received horrible news. Is it your father? Your mother? One of your siblings?'

He pressed his mouth together so flatly his lips turned white. He swung his legs over the bed and stood, still gripping his phone. 'There's been a press leak.' He let out a hissing breath. 'About us.'

This time it was Holly's turn to swallow. 'What does it say?'

His expression was so rigid with anger, she could see

every muscle outlined as if carved in stone. 'It's not so much what it says as what it shows.'

Her stomach dropped. 'There are pictures? Of us?'

He scraped a hand through his hair. 'Yes.'

'Show me.'

'No.'

Holly got off the bed and held out her hand for his phone. 'Show me.'

He held the phone out of her reach, his face so tortured with anguish her heart squeezed. 'No, Holly. Please. It's best if you don't. I'll make it go away. I'll get my lawyer onto it.'

Her eyes widened. '*Your lawyer*? Surely they can't be that bad. How did anyone get photos of us? We haven't been out together in public.'

Julius was looking so ashen Holly felt sick to her stomach. She took the phone from him. This time he didn't fight her for it. It was like he was stunned. Shocked into inertia. She clicked on his most recent message. It was from his twin brother with a short message— WTF?—with a link to a press article with two pictures. They were erotic, almost pornographic shots of her and Julius making love in the pool.

Her mouth went dry. Dry as sandpaper. She couldn't get her voice to work. All she could think was how horrible this was for Julius. How shaming. How mortifying. Someone had captured them in their most intimate moments and splashed it all over the world's media. The media Julius did everything in his power to avoid. *This* was what she had brought to his life. *She* had done this to him. She knew exactly who was behind that long-range camera lens. This was how it was always going to be. She could never have a normal life. Not while her stepfather was alive. He would hunt her down. He would destroy her and anyone she dared to care about.

'I can make it go away,' Julius said into the canyon of silence.

Holly began collecting her things and stuffing them haphazardly into the backpack she had stored in his wardrobe.

'What are you doing?'

'I'm leaving.'

'You can't leave.'

She slung the straps of her backpack over one shoulder. 'I have to leave, Julius. I reckon I've caused enough trouble for you. I admit I wanted to when I first arrived, but even by my standards this is going too far.'

He frowned so hard his brows met over his eyes. 'You don't think I'm blaming *you* for this?'

'It's my fault,' Holly said. 'I've done this to you because I do this kind of stuff to the people I care about. I wreck their lives. I stuff up everything for them just by breathing.'

'You care about me?'

Holly mentally bit her tongue. 'I'm not in love with you, if that's what you're asking.'

'I don't believe you,' he said. 'You *do* love me. That's why you're running away like a spooked rabbit. You're too frightened to let me handle this. You want to trust me to keep you safe when no one's ever been able to do it before. But I *can* keep you safe, Holly. You have to trust me. I will *not* allow anyone to hurt you.'

Holly wanted to believe him. She ached to believe he cared enough to sacrifice his privacy, his reputation and even his family for her. But she wasn't worth it. She knew he would come to resent her for it. The press would never leave them alone. Her stepfather would see to it. Her stepfather would taint their relationship. He would sully it. Cheapen it.

And ultimately destroy it.

'I don't think you're listening to me, Julius,' Holly said. 'I don't *want* to stay. I wouldn't stay if you paid me to. I've got plans. I'm not changing them. My future is in England; it's not here with you.'

His mouth tightened. His hands clenched and un-clenched by his sides. Holly got the feeling he was at war with himself. Fighting back the impulse to reach for her. 'Fine,' he said at last. 'Leave. I'll call Natalia and get her to pick you up. You won't be able to leave the country until your community service time is up.'

Holly knew it would be the longest three days of her life.

Julius stood in a stony silence as Holly was driven away by her caseworker. It felt as if his heart was tied to the rear of the car. The tugging, straining, gutting sensation took his breath away. He was sure she was lying and yet…and yet what if he was wrong? What if she had set him up from the start? She was a troublemaker. A rebel. She had openly admitted to wanting to make his life dif-ficult. He thought back to the pool. Both times she had lured him out there…hadn't she? It had been her idea to make love out there. It wasn't something he would normally do. She was always poking fun at his conser-vative nature. Was that why? So she could set him up and shame him the in the most shocking way possible?

But then he thought of how she had trusted him enough to tell him about the horrible stuff that had happened to her as a child. That wasn't an act. She had the scars to prove it. Her stepfather was behind this photo scandal. He had to be. Julius just had to prove it.

If he could make Holly feel safe by seeing justice served then maybe, just maybe, she would trust him enough to admit to her feelings.

He reached for his phone and called a close friend, Leandro Allegretti. Leandro was a forensic accountant who occasionally did some work for Jake's business analysis company. They had gone to school together and Leandro had spent many a weekend or holiday at Ravensdene while they'd been growing up. If anyone could uncover secrets and lies, it was Leandro. He made it his business to uncover fraud, money laundering and other white-collar crime.

'Leandro?' Julius said. 'Yeah, it's me. Listen, I have a little project for you...'

Holly had finally made it to England. She had found a tiny flat in central London and even landed a job in a deli, which should have made her feel as if all her boxes were ticked, but she felt miserable. The weather was freezing, for one thing. And it never seemed to stop raining. She had spent years dreaming of the time when she would be here, doing normal stuff like normal people, and yet she felt lost. Empty. Hollow. As if something was missing. Even the shops didn't interest her. She hadn't heard from Julius, but then she didn't expect to, not really. She had cut him from her life in the only way she knew how. Bluntly. Permanently.

But she missed him. She missed everything about him. The security she felt when she was with him was only apparent to her now it had been taken away. She had felt *safe* with him. Now she was anchorless. Like a paper boat bobbing about in the middle of the ocean.

Holly was on a tea break in a nearby café when she

flicked through the day's newspaper and her eyes honed in on an article that was only a couple of paragraphs long about a recent criminal charge in Argentina. Her eyes widened in shock when she saw her stepfather's name cited as the man at the centre of the investigation that had uncovered a money-laundering and drug-running scheme that had gone on for over twenty years.

Holly sat back in her seat with a gasp of wonder. It had finally happened. Franco Morales's lawyer said his client had pleaded guilty and bail was denied. How had that come about? Who was behind it? Who had shone the light of suspicion on her stepfather?

A cramped space inside Holly's chest suddenly opened. *Julius*. Of course he would have gone after her stepfather. Hadn't he promised he would not allow anyone to hurt her? He had been true to his word. He had taken on one of Argentina's most notoriously elusive criminals and brought about justice. *For her.*

Holly shot out of her seat. She had to see him. She had to see him to thank him in person. To tell him... what? She sat back down in her seat. Huddled back into her coat. She didn't belong in his world. How could she? She worked in a deli. She had no qualifications. He was the son of London theatre royalty.

And his mother hated her.

'Is this seat taken?'

Holly looked up to see a woman standing next to the empty chair on the opposite side of the table. She looked vaguely familiar but Holly couldn't quite place her. Maybe she had served her in the shop in the past week or so. 'No; I'm leaving soon, in any case.'

The woman sat down. 'You don't recognise me, do you?'

Holly blinked as the woman took off her sunglasses. Why anyone would be wearing sunglasses on such a miserably wet day in London had occurred to her but then she figured it took all types. Now she realised it was all part of a disguise. A very clever one, too. No one would ever guess Elisabetta Albertini would frequent a humble little café in Soho dressed like a bag lady. 'No,' Holly said. 'Even your accent is different. But then, I guess you can do just about any accent.'

Elisabetta gave her a sly smile. 'So, how's London working out for you?'

'Great. Fine. Brilliant.'

'You'd better stick to your day job,' Elisabetta said. 'You're a terrible actor.'

Holly grimaced. 'Yeah, I know. But I hate my day job. I don't want to do this for the rest of my life. Nor do I want to be cleaning up after people.'

'What did you want to be when you were a little girl?'

'I wanted to be a kindergarten teacher—but why are you even asking me this after the way you spoke to me at Julius's? And how did you find me?'

'Julius told me.'

Holly frowned. 'But how does he know where I am?'

'He made it his business to find out,' Elisabetta said. 'Look, I was wrong to speak to you the way I did. Richard's parents did the same thing to me all those years ago when he brought me home to introduce me to them. They made me feel so worthless. I swore I would never treat any daughter-in-law of mine like that, but then I went and did it to you.'

'Daughter-in-law?' Holly said, frowning harder. 'No one said anything about marriage. We had a fling, that's all, and now it's over.'

'He loves you, Holly,' Elisabetta said. 'He'll want to marry you because that's his way. Jake would be another thing entirely. But with Julius you can be assured he'll always do the right thing.'

Holly narrowed her eyes. 'Did he *make* you come here to apologise to me?'

Elisabetta gave her a coy look. 'Does it matter? If he's going to marry you, then I'm going to have to accept it or lose him.'

Holly's frown deepened another notch. 'He shouldn't have done that. You're his mother. He's lucky to have you. I wish I had a mother. I have no one. No one at all.'

Elisabetta put her hand over Holly's and gave it a light squeeze. 'I'm not the best mother in the world. I know that, and it upsets me if I allow myself to think about it, so I don't think about it.' She pulled her hand away as if she had a time limit on touch and sat back in her seat. 'But who knows? Maybe I'll do a better job as a mother-in-law.'

'You mean you wouldn't...*mind*?'

Elisabetta gave a short but not very pleasant-sounding laugh. 'Of course I mind. But I'm an actor; I'll pretend I don't. But don't tell Julius. It can be our little secret.'

Holly gave her a telling look. 'You won't be able to fool him no matter how brilliant an actor you are.'

The older woman's gaze was suddenly very direct. 'Do you love my son?'

Holly gave a heartfelt sigh. 'So much it hurts to think I might never see him again.'

Elisabetta smiled a mercurial smile and popped her sunglasses back on as she got up to leave. 'I have a feeling you'll be seeing him very soon. *Ciao.*'

Holly gathered her things and made to get up but a tall

shadow fell over her. She looked up to see Julius standing there, beads of rain clinging to his cashmere coat, his hair and even to the ends of his eyelashes. 'I know my mother's a hard act to follow, but here I am. Did she apologise?'

'Yes…' Holly licked her suddenly dry lips. Maybe now wasn't the right time to talk about his mother's 'apology'. 'I can't believe what you did for me. It was… amazing. Unbelievable. I can never thank you enough.'

'There is one way,' he said. 'Will you do me the honour of becoming my wife?'

Holly thought her heart was going to burst out of her chest cavity with sheer joy. Could this really be happening? 'Why me? You could have anyone. I'm no one.'

He took her by the hands and gripped them tightly. 'You're everything to me. Everything. I love you, Holly. More than I can ever tell you. I know this isn't a dream proposal. In fact, I can't believe I'm proposing to you in a public place—but I can't bear another moment without knowing you'll agree to spend the rest of your life with me. You don't have to come back to Argentina if you don't want to. I can move back to England.'

Holly looked at him in stunned surprise. 'You'd do that for me?'

'Of course.'

She wrinkled her nose. 'But the weather's foul.'

'I know, but at least we could cuddle up in bed,' he said with a glint in his eyes.

Holly grinned back. 'I guess we could split the time between here and there. Summer here, winter there.'

'Sounds like a good plan to me,' he said, drawing her close. 'I missed you so much. I never realised what a boring life I've been living until you came into it.'

Holly felt the sting of happy tears at the back of her eyes. 'I was miserable from the moment I got on that plane. I'd planned that moment for years. I'd looked forward to it. Counted the days, the hours, even the minutes. But as soon as we took off I felt empty. As if I was leaving a part of myself behind.'

Julius blotted a tear that had escaped from her left eye. 'Do you love me or have I been deluding myself?'

Holly held his hand against her cheek. 'I love you. I'm not sure when I started. Maybe when you took me out on the balcony. You were so kind and patient. I didn't stand a chance after that.'

He smiled a tender smile. 'So will you marry me, my darling?'

Holly wanted to pinch herself to check she wasn't dreaming. 'No one's ever proposed to me before.'

'Lucky me to be the first.'

Holly put her arms around his waist and smiled as his mouth came down towards hers. 'Lucky us.'

* * * * *

If you've loved stepping into the world of
THE RAVENSDALE SCANDALS, *you won't want to miss the next sizzling instalment in this thrilling new quartet!*

AWAKENING THE RAVENSDALE HEIRESS
by Melanie Milburne—available January 2016
from Harlequin Presents!

MILLS & BOON®
Hardback – December 2015

ROMANCE

The Price of His Redemption	Carol Marinelli
Back in the Brazilian's Bed	Susan Stephens
The Innocent's Sinful Craving	Sara Craven
Brunetti's Secret Son	Maya Blake
Talos Claims His Virgin	Michelle Smart
Destined for the Desert King	Kate Walker
Ravensdale's Defiant Captive	Melanie Milburne
Caught in His Gilded World	Lucy Ellis
The Best Man & The Wedding Planner	Teresa Carpenter
Proposal at the Winter Ball	Jessica Gilmore
Bodyguard...to Bridegroom?	Nikki Logan
Christmas Kisses with Her Boss	Nina Milne
Playboy Doc's Mistletoe Kiss	Tina Beckett
Her Doctor's Christmas Proposal	Louisa George
From Christmas to Forever?	Marion Lennox
A Mummy to Make Christmas	Susanne Hampton
Miracle Under the Mistletoe	Jennifer Taylor
His Christmas Bride-to-Be	Abigail Gordon
Lone Star Holiday Proposal	Yvonne Lindsay
A Baby for the Boss	Maureen Child

MILLS & BOON®
Large Print – December 2015

ROMANCE

The Greek Demands His Heir	Lynne Graham
The Sinner's Marriage Redemption	Annie West
His Sicilian Cinderella	Carol Marinelli
Captivated by the Greek	Julia James
The Perfect Cazorla Wife	Michelle Smart
Claimed for His Duty	Tara Pammi
The Marakaios Baby	Kate Hewitt
Return of the Italian Tycoon	Jennifer Faye
His Unforgettable Fiancée	Teresa Carpenter
Hired by the Brooding Billionaire	Kandy Shepherd
A Will, a Wish…a Proposal	Jessica Gilmore

HISTORICAL

Griffin Stone: Duke of Decadence	Carole Mortimer
Rake Most Likely to Thrill	Bronwyn Scott
Under a Desert Moon	Laura Martin
The Bootlegger's Daughter	Lauri Robinson
The Captain's Frozen Dream	Georgie Lee

MEDICAL

Midwife…to Mum!	Sue MacKay
His Best Friend's Baby	Susan Carlisle
Italian Surgeon to the Stars	Melanie Milburne
Her Greek Doctor's Proposal	Robin Gianna
New York Doc to Blushing Bride	Janice Lynn
Still Married to Her Ex!	Lucy Clark

MILLS & BOON®
Hardback – January 2016

ROMANCE

The Queen's New Year Secret	Maisey Yates
Wearing the De Angelis Ring	Cathy Williams
The Cost of the Forbidden	Carol Marinelli
Mistress of His Revenge	Chantelle Shaw
Theseus Discovers His Heir	Michelle Smart
The Marriage He Must Keep	Dani Collins
Awakening the Ravensdale Heiress	Melanie Milburne
New Year at the Boss's Bidding	Rachael Thomas
His Princess of Convenience	Rebecca Winters
Holiday with the Millionaire	Scarlet Wilson
The Husband She'd Never Met	Barbara Hannay
Unlocking Her Boss's Heart	Christy McKellen
A Daddy for Baby Zoe?	Fiona Lowe
A Love Against All Odds	Emily Forbes
Her Playboy's Proposal	Kate Hardy
One Night...with Her Boss	Annie O'Neil
A Mother for His Adopted Son	Lynne Marshall
A Kiss to Change Her Life	Karin Baine
Twin Heirs to His Throne	Olivia Gates
A Baby for the Boss	Maureen Child